Danger Woman

A Botswana Mystery

Frederick Ramsay

Poisoned Pen Press

Copyright © 2016 by Frederick Ramsay

First Edition 2016

10 9 8 7 6 5 4 3 2 1

Library of Congress Catalog Card Number: 2015949432

ISBN: 9781464205859   Hardcover
      9781464205873   Trade Paperback

Poisoned Pen Press
6962 E. First Ave., Ste. 103
Scottsdale, AZ 85251
www.poisonedpenpress.com
info@poisonedpenpress.com

Printed in the United States of America

This, the last in the Botswana Trilogy,
is dedicated to our Botswana family:

Jeff, and Sekgabo; Alex, Oatile, and Kopano.

Acknowledgments

Again, I want to express my sincere thanks to my publisher, editor(s) and the staff of Poisoned Pen Press for their encouragement and patience.

Frederick Ramsay, 2016

Chapter One

A near moonless night, made more uncomfortable for the people crammed into the SUV, by being parked so close to a pack of circling and yapping hyenas. Few sights are spookier or potentially more dangerous than the bright eyes of a pack of spotted hyenas encountered at close quarters at night. Through bulky night vision goggles, they tracked the animal's movements, all of which seemed to be part of an innate and undecipherable choreography. Ole Andersen turned to the two couples in the back of his battered Land Rover.

"Kleptoparasitism," he said. He pointed to his right and toward a pack of spotted hyenas harassing a lone lioness. She had a Thompson's gazelle under her front paws and fangs bared, snarled at the hyenas. "It is where one predator steals the prey of another, usually a weaker predator. Tonight they have taken on a lion, which is unusual, but not rare. It wouldn't happen if this was a leopard. She would have dragged her kill up into a tree and thus, no hyena attacks. In this case, you see, if these hyenas are lucky, if the lion thinks they might attack her in force, she will give up her prize and they will take it. There, you see, she is not so sure. A single hyena will not dare attack a lion. Not even two or three, but if a critical mass is reached…who knows. Look, you see the somewhat larger hyena on the left? That is the dominant female. Remember what I told you earlier? Hyenas are matriarchal and the *alpha* will be female. The game rangers call her Kotsi Mosadi. It means dangerous woman. They like to call her Danger Woman."

His passengers, board members from Denmark, decked out in too-new bush jackets and cargo pants and shorts, twisted in their cramped seats to view the animal that Ole wished them to see. They smiled politely at what they took to be quaint native nomenclature—Danger Woman. They were in the country to observe and report back to the foundation that funded Ole's research. They served as trustees on that board and they were to be indulged. He wondered if they weren't secretly wishing they were comfortably ensconced in the bar or back in their beds at the Marina Lodge and not wedged into the rear of his cramped ancient Land Rover. They adjusted their night vision goggles and watched the standoff unfold. Two more hyenas trotted up and joined the group, then two more. This addition apparently created the critical mass needed to alter the balance of power. The lion hesitated, seemed to consider the odds against her, took one final swipe with a paw at her tormentors, turned, and trotted away, ceding the gazelle to the yapping and snarling melee of scruffy hyenas.

"There, you see, kleptoparasitism." Ole spoke with the accents of his native Denmark although he hadn't lived there in over forty years. Fresh from his graduate studies in Copenhagen he'd been invited to Southern Africa to study wildlife. He'd fallen in love with its exotic beauty and had never returned. Over the ensuing years, he'd made a life for himself, married a local woman, a Motswana, lost her to tuberculosis, and raised a daughter alone. In a country still dealing with widespread HIV, raising a girl created more worries for a parent. His sister insisted that he return to Denmark. Africa, she knew to be a dangerous place and not one suitable to bringing up a child. After giving it some serious thought, he'd refused. In spite of all the personal distractions year after year, he'd managed to raise his daughter to womanhood, acquire a series of research grants that allowed him to settle in the country permanently, and in the end become one of the world's better known experts in hyena behavior.

The hyenas had no interest in Ole, his guests, or his research. They milled around the gazelle, barking and chortling, the sound that had given them their misnomer, laughing hyenas. In their mad and competitive rush to feed, they crashed through the dry bush and dragged the gazelle several meters to one side. The three observers shifted in the seat to mark the progress of the snarling animals as they chased the carcass across the stubble. Not all of the hyenas moved. Ole shifted his gaze back to the area where the lioness and her prize had been to see what held the remaining hyenas in place.

The gazelle's body had previously blocked from sight whatever lay there before. Either the lion had been busy or something else had. Ole peered closer and cursed.

"*Kristus!*" He muttered and then, turning to his passengers, apologized. "*Tilgiv mig.*"

He didn't wait to find out if they pardoned his brief lapse into profanity. He put the vehicle in gear and leaned on the horn. Its blare scattered the pack. He had not wanted to do that. He'd spent weeks sitting with Danger Woman's pack, and they had come to ignore his presence. Blowing the horn and disturbing them this way would likely set that effort back a month or more, but he had no choice. A human skull is not a thing you can leave in the park for hyenas to gnaw on. God only knew where the rest of the body might be.

He called the game ranger station. In the dim light, Ole couldn't be sure, but his passengers seemed to have turned green. Maybe it was just the night vision goggles.

When Sanderson received her promotion to superintendent of her district in the Chobe National Park, she'd initiated a policy that required one of her game rangers to be on phone and radio duty twenty-four hours a day. It had been the practice before, but her predecessor had been lax in enforcing it, allowing the duty person to go home and to bed with a live radio. A distress call might or might not have been sufficient to rouse a sleepy game ranger. The result had been several near misses and Sanderson determined that as long as she was in charge, there would be no repeats. She believed the threat of poachers from across the border and, during the dry season, the threat of fire, required that someone should always be available and promptly so.

Her friends would say of her that she took democracy too far. "You are the Supervisor," they said. "You should not draw this all-night duty with the others." But her years as the person who'd been assigned the less pleasant tasks because of her gender and tenure had made her particularly sensitive to the small injustices organizations sometimes impose on some of their members. When she made out the roster for night duty, she diligently added her own name into the rotation. As luck would have it, it was she who took the call from Ole Andersen, "the Hyena Man."

"You are sure of this thing, Mr. Andersen. It is a human skull you are seeing in the bush?"

Assured that it most certainly was, that it could not possibly be a monkey, baboon, or any other animal resident in the park, she signed off with a promise to drive out to meet him. The prospect of a midnight drive through the Chobe National Park did not excite her. The recent rash of deaths, bodies, and their separated parts appearing in her park caused her great concern. Until a few months ago, finding a man or woman in the park in trouble, much less dead, would be a rare thing. But, ever since they found the remains of Rra Botlhokwa, suicide by lion the authorities insisted, these dead people were popping up like fleas on a warthog. She didn't like to think about why that might be. Kgabo Modise, her policeman friend from Gaborone, attributed this morbid activity to a civil war between rivals over control of what passed for corruption in the country generally and the Chobe River District particularly.

"It is the Russian Bratva," he'd declared. "They wish to move into Botswana and if they do, it could spell the end of the clean government we have enjoyed for over a half century." Kgabo had sounded worried and, because she admired this policeman, she worried with him. It seemed with cause. Now she must travel into the park in the dark, find the Hyena Man, and retrieve the head of someone she believed would attract much attention by the police. She would prefer that to be Modise, but it would more likely be the local police and Superintendent Mwambe. He was not a man she had any use for.

She found Ole and took his statement on her newly acquired recording device and sent him and his passengers on their way. She turned on the spotlight mounted on the roof of her vehicle and panned its bright halogen beam in a circle. She saw no evidence of any wildlife still in the area, no glint of luminous eyes staring back at her from the bush. The hyenas would not be far away, though, not with a freshly killed gazelle lying on the ground. Plus the lion Ole said had been there first might linger nearby in hopes of reclaiming her gazelle. Sanderson alit, being careful to first park within a few feet of the skull, donned latex gloves—a present from Modise—and retrieved the head which she placed in a plastic bag, also a present from Modise.

She circled the area once again with her floodlight and then stepped back to the spot where the skull had been lying and focused the beam of her flashlight on the ground nearby. If there was more than this poor head, she did not see it. She would return in the daylight and look again. She recorded her coordinates on her GPS and headed back to the office. She would place the skull in the fridge until morning when she would deposit it with the police. Then, she would return to her home, nap for an hour, sponge off her uniform, and return to work. It promised to be a long day.

Chapter Two

Irena Davidova never succumbed to the despair that finally broke most of the other women forced into the life euphemistically referred to as Moscow Traffic. She managed to retain her sense of self however degrading her nights, her days, indeed her life, had become. An escape from the stench of the gutter became her obsession. This determination to survive did not come without a price. A willingness to accede to the inevitable, no matter how degrading, in order to endure can transform a person into a zombie-like state, a living corpse, or an insensate, angry survivor. For Irena, the choice seemed clear enough: survive. But the mind-numbing abuse and humiliation, the physical and emotional demands on her, meant she had developed an outer shell of unnatural hardness. This sort of life inevitably produced persons with an inordinate coldness of heart and a persona psychologists would describe as "zero affect."

Irena learned not to feel, not to care; to isolate herself and her emotions from the things occurring to her few friends, to her body, to her soul. In the end, even by the implacably brutal standards of the Bratva, she had evolved into a hard woman. But she survived. She survived and thrived, more animal than human, her enemies would say, a scavenger, and a *опасная женщина*, a dangerous woman.

By the time she'd turned eighteen Irena had learned how to manipulate men and decided she would either find a life that afforded her some measure of respect or, with nothing else to lose, die trying. She would not be someone's compliant блудница, *someone's whore*, forever. She would find a safe haven at the least, and if she were lucky, something more than that. But in the dark world she inhabited, that meant securing the protection of men. Men, she learned early on, could be numbered into "button types." One, two, three, and all of the buttons, by which she meant she could attract and lead them by the number of buttons on her blouse she needed to leave unfastened. What she needed, she believed, was a relatively weak one-button man who would melt at the sight of three.

She found him in Oleg Lenka, then a minor Bratva *apparatchik* buried deep in the St. Petersburg organization. As with all men who are intrinsically insecure, Lenka was a braggart, a coward, and an easy conquest for someone like Irena. She saw her chance to mold this man into what he pretended to be and through him climb out of the gutter. It did not take long for Lenka to keep Irena permanently by his side. Then, with Irena's urging, sometimes gentle, often ruthless, he climbed steadily to the top. He gained enough power in the underworld culture to carve out a modest organization of his own. She kept him in tow with her skills learned in the bedrooms of the rich and famous and the less so. A university professor to whom she'd been leased—that was how she thought of it: she was for rent—described her talents as her "womanly wiles." He said the words in English and it took her several days to translate them. She liked the thought of having *wiles*. But then she was nothing more than leasehold and she'd determined to move to lease-purchase before age, drugs, or a violent lessee put her in the hospital, on the street, or into an early grave.

Lenka formed his group from an older one whose leader got careless one cold, snowy night in St. Petersburg and was found under the ice in a canal near Nevsky Prospekt the next morning. Lenka carved out a substantial portion of the protection racket in the city, made a shaky alliance with the Bout organization, and turned his attention to other, global opportunities including muscling his way into an air freight operation which moved contraband between one marginal enterprise to another. The United States seemed a likely destination to expand into but he decided it had already become crowded with Moscow gangs, Serbs, Rumanians, and South American drug cartels all vying with an entrenched Mafia. Africa, he decided, or rather Irena had decided for him, would be the next big thing and they would move the main operations there. They were not alone in their estimation. The Chinese, the Yakuza, and other Bratva groupings also saw the Dark Continent as a fertile ground to plant new organizations. So, while Western Democracies dithered over their policies about Africa, the several global undergrounds moved inexorably in, prepared to create significant problems for those diplomats when they finally decided that there were important issues to be addressed there.

The natural resources which had sustained European exploitation in the past were now available to anyone bold enough to go after them. By the time Lenka arrived, others had secured most of Central and North Africa. He joined the mad rush to settle in Southern Africa, which by most people's standards should be easy pickings. Lenka managed to garner a small foothold in Cape Town, South Africa's most European and therefore welcoming city.

Irena turned him toward Botswana. Other players specializing in crime and corruption had adopted a wait-and-see position with that country. Its main resource, diamonds, was firmly under governmental control and regulation. There would be no "Conflict Diamonds" to be had in Botswana, not easily anyway. The country seemed determined to resist any and all efforts to introduce even petty graft into its political system, a necessary precursor to any real takeover. Almost everyone agreed it was only a matter of time until Western progress would reach a level where corruption could flourish. The more conservative criminal elements determined to wait. There was more than enough to keep them busy in Johannesburg.

Irena had not survived her life before Lenka by being passive. She knew that the first one in could call all of the subsequent shots and so, while others spent their time in organizing efforts in Johannesburg and Pretoria, she set her lover's eyes northward. Like Joshua in the Bible, she made sure scouts were dispatched into the land, to Gaborone. They reported that while it might be difficult, there appeared to be enough willing players to mount a small effort in that city. Small-time criminals and small-time crime, promising in the long run, a chance to establish a foothold, at least, and a platform on which to build. That done, she turned her eyes farther northward.

She heard about the casino built by an American on the Chobe River. She and Lenka traveled there as tourists. They talked to people, discovered the local soft spot in the otherwise straight society. Rra Botlhokwa, the local "Mr. Big," ran a small-time graft, smuggling, and contraband operation. It was rumored he had a back door relationship with the Intelligence Community, but that had never been confirmed. Lenka sent operatives who proceeded to remove Botlhokwa and any members of his loosely defined organization who had second thoughts about cooperating with the new order. He would steal the old man's business, "Lock, stock, and barrel," he'd said. Lenka believed his mastery of the English language and it many colloquialisms set him apart from his rivals. Kleptoparasitism was not in his lexicon or he would have said that instead.

The process had not been as easy as he had assumed. There were others in the field by then, some with the backing of his mother country, some not. The Nigerians with their ability to "blend in," remained a particular problem. Not an insurmountable one, but real, nonetheless. The Chobe River with its high-end tourists, hotels, and a nascent casino represented too big a plum to have gone unnoticed. At the moment a small, but grisly civil war raged in the dark. People had to choose, competition had to be discouraged, and consequently the number of deaths occurring in the north seemed to skyrocket overnight. How large that number might actually be was masked by the vastness of the Chobe National Game Park and its adjoining river, with its always-hungry animal life. A body dropped in either might never be found, a convenience Lenka likened to the legendary landfills of early-twentieth-century New Jersey.

The fact that the first attempt had been marked by the killing of a local police officer and the arrest of one of his operatives should have worried Lenka. But he foolishly assumed that what worked in St. Petersburg also worked in Africa. That a life in a country fighting an AIDS epidemic would be less valued than elsewhere, that brutality and terror would sway any culture, and so he did not worry about what he considered a small bump in his road to criminal dominance.

He should have.

Chapter Three

Sanderson gathered up Charles Tlalelo and headed to the car park. "We are going to search for bones and I need you to help," she said, and handed him a GPS device.

One dared not venture alone into the park on foot or with the intention of leaving one's vehicle for more than a few seconds. The park spread out over thousands of acres and the chance a lion or other predator might lurk behind the nearest bush, while remote, was still a possibility. Few, if any humans, would be quick enough to avoid its powerful paws and jaws if encountered. Sanderson wanted Charles to keep watch and, if necessary, fire his rifle in the air to frighten off any predators which might venture too close. Charles jumped at the chance to leave his desk and paperwork behind. Sorting through census figures of the numbers and kinds of species in the park served an important function, but also remained an extremely dull occupation for someone yearning to be a man of importance. He stood, tucked in the tail of his uniform shirt, put on his aviator sunglasses, and headed for the door. Sanderson had him set the coordinates on her GPS device to those she'd recorded the previous night.

It took a little under a half hour to find the spot. She circled the area three times in decreasing concentric circles and, handing the rifle to Charles, got out of the SUV. It would soon be warm and the animals would seek what shade the bush offered. She scanned the surroundings with great care. The area seemed safe enough. The hyenas had returned and reduced the gazelle to unrecognizable bits and pieces. Unlike most of their competitors, the big cats, hyenas use their incredibly powerful jaws to crack and chew through bone. Whereas a cat or vultures would strip off the meat and soft body parts and usually leave a bloody skeleton behind, a hyenas left only pieces that required a trained eye to reassemble into an identifiable kill.

As she expected, she found nothing much that she could identify with any certainty. A medical examiner would have to do that. But there were two distinct areas and the fragments were obviously from separate victims. The size of the bones, one she believed to be the head of a femur, suggested she'd found what little remained of the rest of the body that went with the head. Satisfied she had all that was possible, she bagged what she could, tossed them into the rear of the Land Rover, and climbed into the passenger seat.

"Very well, Charles, let us go on a treasure hunt."

"Pardon?"

"The park, as you must be aware of by now, has become a dumping ground for the bodies of all sorts of people who must be in this struggle for the late Rra Botlhokwa's business. I want to see if we have all or if we might have missed a body or two."

"How will we do that, Sanderson? Has the Lord provided you with a map?"

"*Manong*, Charles. We will look for the vultures who will worry a carcass for weeks if they have no new supply of death to feast on. As the priest says to us on Sunday, turn your eyes heavenward and look for a sign. So yes, you could say that *Modimo* has given us a map. *A re tsamaye,* and put on your hat. The sun is very strong here and I do not want to lose you to the heat. "

Charles did as he was told but realized the aviator glasses did not present so well with his hat in place. "Okay, okay, I'm right behind you."

They spent the rest of the morning contemplating the sky, looking for *manong* and any other sign that something had been killed and still held what Sanderson thought of as forensic interest. They saw only a few vultures while wheeling through wadis and the bush, but they did find, quite by chance—no vultures overhead—another partial skeleton. More importantly, the remains included a wallet which contained an ID and photos. Termites had destroyed the leather that had faced the ground, but had not made it past the first ten pula note in the billfold.

An ID would be important, for sure. They drove back to headquarters. Before she turned the wallet over to Mwambe's people, Sanderson would have Charles photograph it and all of its contents. It wasn't that she didn't trust the fat police superintendent, but in the past she had witnessed him drop his gear box into low when evidence of a crime he did not wish to deal with found its way into his presence. She would have copies just in case. In case of what she couldn't say, but she would have them made anyway.

Superintendent Mwambe did not appear pleased at the sight of Sanderson. For him, trouble cropped up every time this woman crossed his path. Today nothing had changed. His forensic people called to say that the woman game ranger had dropped by and they had a badly mauled human skull to deal with. They further informed him that she intended to search the park for the rest of the body and any others that might be lying out in the bush and would bring what she found to them as well.

Mwambe sighed. All this killing would soon bring the authorities up from Gaborone to his post and that meant once again Sanderson would be responsible for drawing unwanted attention to his jurisdiction. Not a good beginning for his day. He sent his nephew Derek out for coffee and a meat pie. He would have a second breakfast.

A morose Yuri Greshenko sat at the small table in the casino coffee shop staring at a cold cappuccino. He'd come to Botswana as an assistant to Leo Painter, the rich American who thought he'd need Yuri's special skills as a former Russian gang member to forward his project. Yuri had agreed to accompany the American industrialist for reasons of his own. Painter had called it a win-win. Yuri would find a new life and Leo would have the leverage he'd need against any rivals who might have been lurking in the darker recesses of Botswana's underworld. As it happened there were few and Yuri's special talents had not been required.

So, the American had been right after all—win-win. Almost. He'd believed he had a chance at a new start. Now, Yuri wasn't so sure. His past had caught up with him. The police had found him out and deemed him an undesirable. He would have to leave or else. The *or else* involved working for them to sniff out a new threat from abroad, a Russian group of gangsters, more accurately, Bratva, seemed bent on taking control of the Chobe. Yuri now found himself, like Odysseus, poised between his own Scylla and Charybdis: Serve as a double agent for Botswana's security force, the DIS, or refuse and be shipped back to Mother Russia and inevitably sucked back into the life of a Bratva operative or arrested and jailed on an old warrant. He had believed his clever connection and passage to South-central Africa, a place no one seemed to have heard of, had given him an opportunity to leave that life behind. But it had found him out anyway.

Working for the Bratva had been a life he neither sought nor enjoyed, but as a cast-off army officer in Russia in an economy in transition, he had drifted into it. Once in, he found leaving it alive impossible. Most people did not know that the Bratva, in one form or another, had existed from the time of the Tsars, had endured and even flourished under Communism, then really blossomed to new heights with the unplanned and hasty introduction of capitalism to the old SSRs.

Now, however, and despite his careful maneuvering, it had found him out and he had to choose. The government of Botswana knew about his past and the old but still outstanding warrants for his arrest and did not want him in the country. That is, they did not unless he paid for future hospitality with a favor. Work for them or leave. Either way, his chances of surviving the next step in this journey were slim at best. He'd been outed and consequently, any chance he might have had to return to the U.S. or anywhere outside Russia had evaporated. Fleeing would be futile. One or another of the many agencies on either side of the law would eventually find him. Accepting the offer to spy on his former colleagues created its own probable dead end—operative word, dead.

Leo, his patron and now his friend and supporter, sat down opposite him.

"I called everyone I know in Washington," he said and snapped his fingers to draw a waiter's attention. "No dice. They can't help. Can't, won't, damn it. When I ran Earth Global, half of those pussies were on my contribution list, or their boss was. I'm talking millions here, Yuri. You'd think they'd remember and pull a few strings for me."

Before turning the world's second-largest energy and mining company over to new management and retiring, Leo had had his hooks in, and the ear of, most of the movers and shakers in the nation's capital. But in a culture that seemed ruled by *Yes, but what have you done for me lately?,* his stock had plummeted and favors now came few and far between.

"So what do we do now?" he added.

"Do? I have little choices, Leo. Whether I, as you say, fish or cut the bait, I am overboard."

"Lovely mismanaged metaphor, Yuri. You are saying you're screwed."

"Yes, and if screw is the correct, what you say…metaphor, then it is one of those screws that only go one way, that cannot be removed, you know?"

"I don't think hardware is the origin of the expression, but I take your point. So, I ask again, what do you do now?"

"I die quickly or slowly. That is my choice."

"You're being too harsh. Look, the best course for you now is to play along with the local police. Modise is a guy you can trust, I think. Besides, if you do, I have a plan."

"A plan. What plan, Leo? A plan to free me from the Bratva, the police, and who knows what or how many Russian agencies that have me on its list of undesirables?"

"I may have lost my edge with the politicos, but I still have a few cards I can pull out of my sleeve, Yuri. Now drink up. The foreman on this construction job—that's using the term loosely—says he's ready on the west end. We have the new wing to check out. Do you have the punch list or do I?"

Chapter Four

The hyena with the sobriquet Kotsi Mosadi would have rejected the name and the reputation it implied were she capable of conceptual thought which, of course, she was not. She was no more dangerous than any other of her species. Hyenas, male and female, compete with every carnivore in the park, large and small cats, dogs, raptor birds, and even an occasional large insect. Not to do so, and aggressively, would end with either her replacement as the pack leader, the demise of the pack itself, or quite possibly both. The bush is not a place for sentimentality or a Disney personification of wildlife. You may do that in animated movies with casts of cuddly cubs and wise old baboons, but in the park, it was eat or be eaten, be the hunter or be the prey, nothing more, nothing less.

Realistically, hyenas have only two enemies, humans and lions. Either would kill them on sight and both would do so simply out of traditional enmity. That which existed between hyenas and lions was historical and innate, a rivalry that stretched back into the mists of time. But with humans the hatred had been learned, was of more recent origin, and seemed to have more to do with aesthetics than rivalry—they are such unattractive animals. Ancient Egyptians, on the other hand, were said to domesticate hyenas and, like pig farmers of a later era, fatten them and bring to them to market to be eaten, presumably, as a delicacy.

Kotsi Mosadi held the key position in the pack and, to the extent such concepts were to be understood, had responsibilities.

The welfare of her pack, male and female alike, rested on her hunched shoulders. In addition, once a year, she and the other females bore litters ranging from one to four—the young necessary to the pack's survival. If hunting with great success and being a fierce protector of her pack made her dangerous, then so be it, but her behavior differed little from every other leader of spotted hyenas or their smaller, shyer, brown relatives that shared the park. She just happened to be more successful and therefore more obvious to the game rangers charged with monitoring her behavior. In truth, Kotsi Mosadi, was spoken of by them more in admiration than contempt.

Game rangers are charged with the management of the park and its denizens. Poachers, intruders of all sorts whose intentions are less than beneficial to the animals, are pursued aggressively and punished severely when caught. That would include any attempt to hurt Danger Woman. Lions, however, were given a pass should they manage to hunt her down and dispatch her. And given half a chance, they would do that. For her part, a sick or weakened lion would be fair game. The difference between them: the lion would never deign to eat a hyena, while a hyena will eat anything, including an unlucky lion.

From the relative shade of the bush she stirred from her midday doze. With those of her pack who were also awake, she watched Sanderson's Land Rover bounce by and pause while its occupants inspected a pile of bones. The hyena's interest would not be piqued as long as nothing emerged from the vehicle. To Danger Woman and her pack, the larger thing represented an entity too big to attack, something akin to a noisy and smelly elephant. However, in her experience, occasionally smaller, and more easily attacked things sometimes emerged from within and could be targeted if they strayed too far from the big one. That would be at night. Daylight was not the hunting time for hyenas. She blinked as the small thing emerged, gathered bones, and then disappeared back into the big creature again. Kotsi Mosadi had no interest in those bones. She knew they were dried out and contained few nutrients.

It would be dark soon enough and then she would lead the pack in hunting. Even though she'd fed the night before on the lioness' gazelle, she would need to eat again and soon. The pups in her womb were growing and their demands on her body for sustenance grew with them. She longed for a dead elephant to scavenge. The pack could eat for weeks on a moderately large elephant.

◇◇◇

"Be careful, Sanderson," Charles Tlalelo said and glanced toward the bush. "*Dipheri* are lurking over there. I think it must be Kotsi Mosadi and her pack. She would quickly separate you from your life if you give her the chance."

"Charles, that hyena is not interested in this middle-aged woman, for sure. I am too tough even for her terrible jaws."

"You are tough, I know, but I am thinking she is tougher and you are not middle aged. My mother is middle aged. She looks it. You are seeming to be much younger."

"Are you flattering me, Charles?"

"No, I am…never mind. Just be careful."

Sanderson grinned. The bones had been picked clean and sometime in the past, which explained why the hyenas dozed a few meters away instead of protecting a possible meal. She brushed aside the twigs and bits of grit and placed them into a plastic bag which she then tossed into the back of the Land Rover.

"Next stop, the office and lunch, Charles. We have made progress. I wonder who this poor soul was before he or she became someone's dinner."

Charles put the SUV into gear and they headed for the main gate to the park. Two safari trucks with rows of tourists perched in tiers, cameras at the ready, waited while their driver/guides cleared the vehicles with the attendant.

"Let us hope none of these eager people decides to hop out of the truck to retrieve a hat or camera and become a lion's midday meal."

Charles looked worried. "Has that ever happened, Sanderson?"

"Almost. People see the lions lolling in the grass like big pussies and they forget that they can weigh hundreds of kilos and are always hungry. They would probably love a belly rub from some plump tourist, but I am sure they would prefer fresh meat more. Elephants, too. These visitors think they are visiting Babar and then some great bull in musk, or for no reason at all, decides their truck is too close, the horn beeping too loud, it is a threat to the calves, or who knows why, and topples their car and possibly crushes them. Over in the Okavango Delta they have bigger problems because the people camp in the park and will sometimes think they want an evening stroll out into the wild for a closer look at nature. We will lose a visitor over there now and again."

"That woman in South Africa who wanted to get a close-up of the lioness and left her window down—"

"That was a rarity, Charles, a once in a million, but yes, if the sign says, 'Keep your windows closed,' it is best to do so."

"The park is not a petting zoo."

"Or a playground. Except for the animals, of course."

Chapter Five

As he feared, the discovery of a human skull and other remains, which Sanderson had deposited with the forensics people had attracted the notice of the authorities in Gaborone. An e-mail announcing the imminent arrival of someone from DIS sent the local constabulary scurrying. Superintendent Mwambe sent out for a snack.

"Do they think I am not up to the task?" he asked Derek between bites of chicken sandwich. Derek shrugged. As he owed his position with the local police more to his uncle's beneficence than to his own competence, he was in no position to say. He did know from experience that the people to be sent from Gaborone were far more likely to solve the growing problems in the Chobe than his uncle. Even if the superintendent were the famous Sherlock Holmes himself, this rash of disappearing bad men and body parts turning up in the park was well beyond any one man's capabilities. And his uncle was for sure not Mr. Sherlock Holmes.

"I have been a policeman for thirty years and the superintendent of this district for more than a decade. I never had a... There has never been a single time when I had to have help in doing my job, Derek. Not until this game ranger stuck her woman's nose in. That Sanderson, she is the problem. She is telling them in Gaborone that there is trouble here and they listen to her."

"Um, Uncle, it was the people in forensics who notified the capital. They wanted to have a DNA test done on the bones and the billfold analyzed and we—"

"It was the woman, Derek. That is the fact of the situation. You may believe what you will about who made a call. If you investigate, you will discover it was Sanderson who did this to me."

Mwambe paced the floor, his fists clenched behind his back, a dab of sauce on his upper lip. Somewhere in the distance he heard laughter. Were his men sharing a joke? It made him frown even though he felt sure they were not laughing at him. Or perhaps they were. Had the news reached the ready room and were his officers being amused at his expense? Something had to be done.

"Derek, I am putting you on special assignment."

Derek snapped to attention, or as much as he could manage while sitting down. "Sir?" He wondered what new sort of new trouble his uncle had in store for him now.

"I am assigning you to permanent duty with the game rangers. They will find bodies and so on…Well, that is police business, is it not? I want you to be there and keep a watch, to be a monitor. Find out what this woman is up to and tell me if she has plans."

Botswana is a country about the size of France. Gaborone, its capital, is as far from the Chobe as Calais is from Marseilles. To be stationed in Gaborone and sent north would be considered a major disruption of one's life. Or at least Joseph Ikanya thought so. He stepped out of the director's office. He seemed anxious. No, more than that, distressed. "Old Reliable," as he was called after a rough English translation of his surname from Setswana, was anything but. He had arrived at the level of Inspector due to his time in service. His assignment to the diplomatic sector of the capital had meant he had little need of any particular skill in solving crimes. His job involved traffic control, security patrols, and police escorts. But his name went on the roster with everyone else, and if something special came up he was as likely to draw the assignment as anyone. Today he'd drawn one such—the source of his distress.

What has happened, Joseph? Kgabo Modise had been called to the director's office as well and sat in the anteroom waiting to be called.

"I am to go all the way up to the Chobe on temporary duty?" Ikanya said. "My wife is due any day now and it is her first. My mother-in-law is not so fond of me, you know, and this will not be wonderful news in my house."

"I am sorry, for you, Joseph. I, personally, am very fond of trips to the Chobe."

"Really? But there is nothing of interest up there except tourists and animals."

"It is a beautiful place, Joseph, I assure you. I would go myself if I could. I take my time off there, you know."

"I didn't know. Perhaps you would ask the director if you could take my place."

"He has called me for a meeting just now. I will see what it is he wishes. Why don't you hang around a bit and see?"

The director's door swung open and the director's secretary waved Modise in. The door closed behind Modise, leaving him alone with the director.

"Modise, have a seat," the director said without looking up or taking his eyes from the slim file on the desk in front of him. Modise sat. He knew better than to speak. The director would tell him why he'd been summoned soon enough. His chair was not close enough to the desk for him to make out what the file concerned, but he thought he caught the name Sanderson in the middle of a sentence. So, what had the lovely game ranger gotten into now? The director spun the folder around and motioned for Modise to pull his chair up and look. There was not much to see. Sanderson had found some body parts in the Chobe National Park. Nothing new there. She had found a skull and, as usual, refused to leave it at that. Instead, she had taken it on herself to scour the rest of the park for more evidence of mayhem and murder. Modise smiled. He knew this woman and realized she had not changed much in spite of his constant urging to stay with her job and leave policing to the police. "Stay in your lane," he'd said the last time they'd spoken.

The director drummed his fingers on the desk. He lit a cigarette, stared at it in disgust, and then snuffed it out. "You have worked with this Sanderson person in the past. Am I correct in thinking this?" The director fixed Modise with his laser look. It meant that Modise would be wasting his time skirting questions of any sort from this point forward.

"Yes, sir."

"More than just work with her, I am told."

"She is a…friend, sir."

"A friend? Yes. Well, that is good. My spies tell me she also oversteps her duties and sometimes anticipates the Superintendent of Police in Kasane."

"Anticipates? Ah yes, perhaps so. She has a curious nature, sir." He could not be certain but Modise thought he saw a smile flit across the director's face. It did not last long enough for him to estimate its significance.

"A curious nature. Very well put, Modise. Well, to the point. I am sending Ikanya up there to liaise with this Mwambe person."

"Sir, I…"

"Yes?"

"Sorry, nothing. You were saying Joseph is to go to Kasane and work with Superintendent Mwambe."

"Precisely. My reading on both of them is that they are not the quickest baboons in the congress, if you follow. I want Ikanya to spend his time diverting the superintendent while you sort out this business in the park. The news services have not yet tumbled to the fact that the park has become a graveyard for our less than noble citizens and it is important that they never do. We depend on a thriving tourist business up there in the Okavango Delta and in the Chobe."

"Yes, sir. Ah, you were aware Ikanya's wife is due to have their first baby soon. I think he worries he will not be available to—"

"Is that what he told you? The woman is in her seventh month. She will not surprise him anytime soon and I need his inept presence in the Chobe. Now, you also know we have suborned a Russian national into our service?"

"Yuri Greshenko, yes."

"You will run him. The deal we have with Mr. Greshenko is, he works for us and he doesn't get deported to Russia. His choices are not good and he will not be happy, but he knows we have him."

"Then you believe the Russian Bratva is, in fact, making a play into the Chobe?"

"We are sure of it. This man Lenka has sent his scouts. They have begun to recruit—negatively and positively, you could say. We need to shut him down before he firms up his foothold."

"Yes, sir. Where should I start?"

"With Ranger Sanderson. Work with her. She, it seems, has a better grasp of the park and the area than anyone and…there is one more thing you should know."

"Sir?"

"We sent Bahiti Ditlalelo up there undercover. We didn't hear from him for nearly two weeks. Then Ranger Sanderson found his wallet in the park near some bones. Modise, they know we're on to them so, be very careful."

Chapter Six

Kgabo Modise had attained the position he now held as much by his work ethic as his intelligence. He was bright, no doubt about that; in a developing country, sometimes that is enough. But Modise also worked hard at his job. His brief, very brief, time with law enforcement agencies in the United States had convinced him that the profession he'd chosen required diligence and patience. The States, he'd discovered, took for granted that people understood the parameters of productivity, and to be unproductive required a conscious decision and effort to be so. New, raw countries, like his, freed from paternalistic overlords, had to learn the how of it. Modise had. And now he realized that he would need to apply those lessons to the case at hand. Law breakers did not reveal themselves; they were to be ferreted out and pursued.

After he left the director's office, carefully avoiding Joseph Ikanya, he returned to his cubicle and rummaged through the stack of documents piled on one of the desk corners. Never throwing anything away had become an important part of his routine. He'd made that mistake once and it had nearly cost him his life. On the other hand, it had resulted in a famously cluttered work area. He extracted a moderately recent file and began to read. He wanted to be sure he had not forgotten anything.

Olegushka Zhoravitch Lenka: *currently a resident of Cape Town, South Africa.*

Lenka has moved between various locales, Sharjah, Antwerp, and Rio de Janeiro. Like his contemporaries, including the presently incarcerated and disgraced Victor Bout, he is a native of the old and the new Russia, the U.S.S.R. as it had been, and the state that now operates in its place. Born in Novograd, educated in St. Petersburg, he emerged as a senior Bratva figure in the late nineties.

His group now operates through multiple fronts including Nexus Aviation which is currently one of the larger commercial air carriers linking Africa, Latin America, Middle East, and Asia. And it has a significant air service infrastructure at O.R. Tambo airport in Johannesburg. Lenka's network linked these services operating out of East Africa, specifically to Uganda and Rwanda, where they apparently are involved in a variety of enterprises in and out of the Democratic Republic of Congo: Specifically guns, spares, drugs, as well as legitimate and quasi-legitimate cargoes such as coltan and, occasionally, conflict diamonds.

His organization employs locals as "boots on the ground" in its markets. In Southern Africa this means the presence of ex-liberation-era combatants both white and black.

Boers, Modise translated. Boers and the riff-raff which flowed across the border from Zimbabwe, all the unhappy people who couldn't get their mind around the fact that Southern Africa was done with killing. He noted the red pencil note he'd added earlier: "How do you fight a gang that has its own air force?"

Next he opened the envelope that had been left for him: Bahiti Ditlalelo's transmissions from the Chobe District before he disappeared.

Lenka is a serious sociopath.

No news there.

He has no sense of basic morality. He will order a killing often simply to make a point and the victim might be chosen at random. He has his eyes on the casino on the Chobe, but that is not all. He believes he can be the Bugsy Siegel of Botswana and build his version of Las Vegas on the river. At this time, I do not see any major financing in place. No "Meyer Lansky" in the background anywhere.

Bahiti knew his American history, at least the criminal part, it seemed.

The best guess is he intends to steal or coerce the present owners of the several hotels and resorts to surrender their control. He is recruiting heavily in the area, with some success. The prosperity promised in the south has not found its way north and the influx of jobless from Zimbabwe makes for easy pickings.

The real threat, though, is the woman, Irena Davidova. She is, I think, the brains behind the operation. If Lenka is cold-hearted, this woman is solid ice.

There was nothing more. Apparently Bahiti had only sent this one piece back before he dropped off the grid. Still, it was useful as far as it went. He would contact Interpol and inquire about this dangerous woman, Irena Davidova.

Kgabo shuffled the sheets of paper and slid them back into his file. A knock on his door. Joseph Ikanya was not to be avoided after all.

"Modise, it is a terrible thing that is happening."

"Joseph, how is this?"

"I must go to the Chobe district and supervise police work there."

"The Chobe is very nice, Joseph. Be glad. The hotels are fine and the food most excellent. Well, you may not enjoy the hotels, I hear. The director is economizing but, in your free time—"

"But, Modise, my wife—"

"She will be fine. I am sure we will be back in Gabz in plenty of time for the new arrival. Is it to be a boy or a girl?"

"I don't know. My wife is superstitious that way. She refuses to discover the truth of this thing. Who is this Superintendent Mwambe I must interface with?"

"Ah. He is the Superintendent of Police in the area. He is old school. You two will get along well, for sure."

"Old school? What does that mean?"

"It means, Joseph, that the two of you will be seeing eye to eye on many important issues. What is it the director wishes you to do?"

"This Mwambe is slow to react, the director says. I am to urge him forward. That does not strike me as a very important thing to be doing."

"You would prefer to be in the field? The problem up there has to do with Russian gangsters fighting with the indigenous criminal element while holding off the Yakuza, the Nigerian gangs, and assorted other would-be successors to the late Rra Botlhokwa's territory."

"But Botlhokwa is dead. He committed suicide they say."

"Suicide by lion, it is reported, yes but…So, the field is wide open for someone else to assume the lead. Botlhokwa ran a loose organization specializing in pretty small stuff. Extortion, smuggling, things like that. If he had an interest in the hotels and that new casino, he hid it pretty well. He is gone and these international elements are moving in. They do not play fair, you could say. Too many bodies are turning up in the game park and that is not good. No, the field is not where a man waiting for his new baby needs to be. Joseph, these criminals must be pinched off in the bud or everything we have worked for as a country will be lost. That is why we need you in Kasane to help the old school policeman."

"Oh, I see." Joseph obviously did not see, but he was at least mollified sufficiently to put his objections aside. "Well, thank you, Modise. That had been most helpful."

"We will fly north together, tomorrow."

"Yes, of course. What will my poor wife be thinking?"

She will be thinking what a relief to get this old hen out of the coop for a while. "She will be fine, Joseph, and proud that you have such important things to occupy you. You will see."

When Joseph Ikanya had cleared the door sill, Kgabo turned his attention back to his own itinerary. He must contact the men and woman already in the field. Personnel that Mwambe did not know about. He would need to put this Russian Greshenko into motion. That could be a problem. How best to use him? How long would he stay alive as a double agent? Not very, he guessed. Too bad about that. Modise remembered him as a nice fellow, his criminal past notwithstanding. How would they know that what he did or said was the truth? The director had not been clear. Would this Russian prefer his own kind and to save his life, betray the police to Lenka's people? This operation is looking like a very risky business. And then there was Sanderson, the beautiful game ranger. What will become of that situation?

So much to do.

Chapter Seven

Moving from east to west, the Mowana Lodge is the first in a string of lodges and resorts that sit on the banks of the Chobe River in Kasane. It has a large baobab tree in the center of its court and decks that face north and the plains of Zambia. During the fire season, one can sit there with a sundowner and watch the smoke from the fires miles away. Tourists ask, "Won't they send the fire department and put them out? What will happen to the animals?" The reply is always the same, "No madam, it is not possible to bring the fire-fighting machines to that area. The fire, he will burn himself out. The animals know what to do."

Irena Davidova and Oleg Lenka occupied two of the chairs on the upper deck. This evening there was no fire to occupy them. It wouldn't have mattered if there had been. They had weightier things to discuss. The Mowana and the other lodges strung out to the west of them, in particular, the new one being built by the American, held their attention. That one had a casino and that one they coveted the most. It would be the postern gate into the castle when they usurped this kingdom, but they needed a plan. The American had a reputation for toughness and probably would not roll over for them. Botswana's police and politicians, they'd discovered, did not respond to their blandishments as their counterparts in St. Petersburg would have done. Irena had been thinking about this for some time.

"It is a simple enough thing, Oleg. You have the man inside, no? This Greshenko is one of us, yes? We use him."

"Wait. He was one of us once, Moscow Bratva, then Chicago. Not so sure anymore he still is."

"Nobody is ever former Bratva, yes? So, we own him either way. He works for us or we turn him over to the local police. If they do not take care of him, he knows what we will do to him. So, he does what we ask."

"Yes, okay. We have Greshenko. So, then what?"

"Listen. This man, Painter, the American. He is old man. He has no close family. Only a daughter who is not happy with him and a wife who does not live here. He is alone. He is not in the best health. He smokes. He drinks. He could die any minute, you see? Who will care what happens to him and even if they do, these people, will they fly from a soft armchair in America to see about a casino in Africa? I don't think so. Not in time, anyway."

"So?"

Irena threw up her hands. "Sometimes, Yuri, I think you have potatoes for brains. Greshenko has this old man sign a paper. That is what he does all the time our man inside says. Greshenko goes to Painter and says, 'here, sign this' and he signs. This time is innocent paper, only later it will be signing over to Greshenko the casino."

"How does that help us? Now the casino is his…wait, why is he signing this paper?"

Irena's eyes rolled upward and around. "He signs paper which is innocent enough, authorizing something. Later, we put more words on it. So, as soon as he signs, he has accident or heart attack and is dead. Greshenko is now owner of casino. If they come from America, so what? The hotel is no longer theirs. They complain, they fuss. Who cares? They go home. Is now only Greshenko owning it and he is working for us or he is also dead. Either way, we have casino and foot in door. Then, one by one, we take the others."

"We will own them?"

Irena shook her head in frustration. "No, owning is too much. No, it will be like everywhere else. Our people will be in their lobby and we take a percentage for 'protection.' Don't you see?

Is the same as in St. Petersburg. Only we have no competition because we are here first."

"And the airline is flying in the high rollers."

"Exactly."

"We will have to kill the American and Greshenko."

"Probably. Is surest way."

"And some others."

"Perhaps others, yes. Is the cost of doing business."

"We cannot buy their police. We have tried. Others, too. There're not enough bananas in the world to buy those monkeys."

"So, we save the money. Have you seen the local police superintendent? He looks like one of those hippos in the river. And he is very slow and stupid like them, too. We will not have to buy him, just flatter him and keep him in meat pies and cheap vodka."

'You're sure of this? He may look funny, but he could be trouble."

"He will be a troublesome policeman when hippos dance, yes?"

"When hippos dance? Oh, you mean like a joke. Very funny. When the hippo dances. Okay, I get it. I still have one worry. Greshenko may not be as easy to run as you think. He was Moscow before he went to the States. They are not an easy group, Moscow. Remember, he helped us one time because he had to. We threatened to turn him over to the local police. I don't think he is stupid and we will need to watch him."

"So, we watch. He will know that and will behave."

"I hope you are right. But think a minute, what if he was not telling the truth about coming here because he is looking to start a new life. Suppose he is here doing the same thing we are? Maybe he is scouting, too."

"It doesn't matter. Did you see anyone else with him? There is the man, Painter, and no one who looks even a little bit like Bratva. We are here, he is alone. One false move and one of those tiresome Boers will be sent to shoot him."

"Maybe."

"Maybe? Why maybe?"

"He is tough and smart. He has to be to have made it this far. I don't think one of those Dutchmen will be able to get the drop on him. If it comes to that, I will send Grelnikov. One tough guy to kill another tough guy. All I am saying, let's hope he isn't the point man for another organization, Bout for instance."

"Bout is history. Forget Bout."

"It is not wise to forget Bout. He is in prison, yes, but he is still connected. He is only a little less dangerous in there than out. But if he wants to, he can still hurt us. I'm just saying we need to be careful, that's all."

Irena puffed her cheeks. Her one-button man still needed some propping up. For now, she would do the propping. Soon, maybe not so soon she would drop this propping. She gave him "the look" and slipped a button. Anticipation has a greater effect on men than the act itself.

"Whatever. Is that a giraffe?"

"Where?"

"Look over there behind those trees. There he is. No, look. There are three of them, a family. See. There is a really tall one, and a not-so-tall one, and the baby. Don't you just love having animals right out where you can see them? Not like a zoo. And these people eat them, right? The…what do you call them…the ones who eat grass? They were on the menu last night. Something beginning with a K. Anyway, when we get settled, Oleg, I want a lion skin rug in the main room."

"Herbivores. You call them herbivores and you can't shoot lions or any game in the park, especially the big cats."

"So, where did the dinner meat come from, Mr. know-it-all?"

"Kudu. It was roasted Kudu. Those are bred like on a farm, or some hunting is allowed with a special permit, I think. I am not so sure, anyway, the people who live on the land keep their right to kill for food, maybe."

"So who's going to stop us, hey? You will be living on the land, too. So you go out there in your truck, find me a lion and shoot him. Somebody will know how to turn him into a rug for the right price. A lion skin and also a zebra for the bedroom. Can you see me on a zebra skin rug? You will get me those?"

Oleg frowned. That was a big order. The image of Irena with her jet black hair and white skin lying naked on a zebra skin rug was arresting, but was making it a reality worth the risk going after this zebra? And never mind the lion. Poaching big game would eventually involve the BDF, the army, and they were rumored to shoot poachers on sight. The President himself was a fierce conservationist and getting caught could end with losing everything they had on their plate. Oleg guessed, rather hoped, that in time she would forget about rugs made from endangered species. If not, he'd find the things on the black market. Surely someone over in Mugabe's country would be happy to provide whatever he, rather she, needed. No way was he going to stir up the BDF.

"Sure, Renee, whatever you want. Another drink?" He snapped his fingers and told the waitress to bring them two more of the same. She was nice looking, for a black woman—fresh. She would bring good money when she changed her profession. That could be soon. Everybody would work for Lenka, or they wouldn't work at all, and what they worked at would be his call. Well, in the case of the women, that would be Renee's call, but this waitress…yes, she would bring in some good money.

Oleg sat back and sighed. Life was good.

Chapter Eight

Patience Botshabelo had been chosen for this particular assignment because of her ability to speak Russian. For a Motswana, that counted as a rarity. Botswana's official language is English, the language of government and commerce. Its native language is Setswana. To be fluent in something as remote as Russian made her an especially useful agent. Her assignment was to listen and learn, to take careful notes about everything the Russians did and, when possible, also what they said. She took the couple's order, left their table to give it to the barman, and slipped well out of their line of sight. She definitely did not like the way the man was looking her over. She had had looks like that since she was old enough to have her bumps, but this man did not give the impression he was only admiring her. He looked like a snake about to swallow a mouse, and she was pretty sure she knew who was the mouse. She retrieved her notebook from her apron and wrote.

Vodka with ice and a twist for the woman, vodka with a beer chaser for Lenka. They always have three drinks before eating. He will always make suggestive remarks to the women who serve in the bar and the restaurant. It is very discomforting to these women. They think he has a bad plan for them. I think they have it right.

The woman is acting like a carnivore on the hunt. What she hunts is not yet clear. They are speaking of making strong steps to take over the casino the American is building. There was some talk of the man Greshenko, but I could not make it out. Something big is planned.

She closed her book, shoved it back in her apron pocket, picked up the drinks and took them back to the couple on the deck. She would stay out of their line of sight but within earshot, if possible. Modise said he would be in Kasane soon and she wanted to report as much as she could. These people were very dangerous, for sure.

❥❥❥

Kgabo Modise and Joseph Ikanya arrived in Kasane mid-afternoon. They booked in the government facility which served as a temporary residence for officials up from the capital and assigned duties in Kasane as well as a "Safe House" for those needing privacy or protection. He would have liked to have a room at one of the lodges, but the director had put an end to that practice when this new facility came online. Modise sent Joseph off to the police post to liaise with Superintendent Mwambe. He dropped his bag on one of the beds in the room assigned to them and found a quiet corner with a desk. He had calls to make, contacts to set up, and plans to implement. Sanderson must be notified of his arrival, too. He had that to look forward to, but first, he needed to check on his agents in the field. He had placed Patience Botshabelo and two other operatives at the Mowana Lodge with instructions to make many notes and listen. She would be first but, as she would not finish her shift until midnight, he would turn his attention to planning what to do with Greshenko. He skimmed the list of other agents placed in the various lodges and likely venues where the Bratva would make their play. It was a thin list. Five people, three women and two men, did not make for much of a task force. Of course there were the local police. They might be useful if he could get Mwambe to stop feeling threatened every time he came to town. He began to call them one by one.

In an hour he had the locations of Lenka, his *nyatsi,* and most of the men thought to have been recruited to his service. Noticeable by their absence were Boers. Lenka had learned his lesson, it seemed, from the last time he tried to make his move on the Chobe. At the moment, there were two bearded and angry

Dutchmen sitting in the cells in Gaborone who would love to cut a deal by giving up their ex-boss, but were too frightened to speak, believing that Lenka's reach extended into the jails. They were correct in this, but it would not be the case soon. That left only two Boers to deal with and while they could be mean and violent, they were not known for brilliance of mind. They should pose no real problem. The director said he had a line on the men involved and still in the city, mostly associated with or hanging around the restaurant which they operated and had named *Ресторан*, which, when said aloud, sounded like, and in fact, meant, restaurant in Russian. Clever.

Kgabo called the American at his casino and arranged a meeting. It was time to infiltrate Lenka's organization and Greshenko was the man to do it.

>>>

Leo Painter thought he knew all of his workmen. It had taken him nearly a year to train his eye to this new environment he had chosen for himself, where at first one face seemed much like every other. He shook his head at the memory. Chagrinned, he's had to admit his own ethnocentric view of the world and pay attention to those around him. He had finally done it. Now he stared at a man shirtless and working a hoe in a large hod of newly mixed concrete.

"Yuri," he asked, "who's the new guy?"

"What new guy? I don't know about any new guy."

Leo pointed out the window to the man wielding the hoe.

"Oh, him. That's one of the cop's people. Modise, you know? He put some people in all of the lodges. That's one of them."

"He's got someone in all of the lodges? I'm impressed. We're not paying this guy, right?"

"I'm not and I don't think you are, so, no. He's on the government's expense account. Should I get rid of him?"

Painter thought a moment. "No. Better to know the devil at hand than the one unseen. Something like that, anyway. If we know who he is, we can watch what we say. Is he the only one?"

"As far as I know, yes. Lenka will have someone in here, too. He shouldn't be too hard to spot either. You said you had a plan."

"I did and I do. We'll wait for Modise to show up and then spring it on him.

"I don't like it, Leo."

"What don't you like? You haven't heard it yet."

"I don't like the idea of trying to trick the cops. They have me by the, what do you say, shorts and I don't want any more bad stuff on my plate. I have too much as it is."

"Faith, Yuri. You must have faith in the enterprising spirit of America. We will not be tricking, as you say, the cops. We will be augmenting their efforts."

"What does that mean, exactly?"

"What does it mean? Well, I, like the Cheshire Cat, will say to you it means whatever I say it means. It's what we believe when we are still in the scheming phase. Nevertheless, trust me, I have this covered."

"I won't even ask what a cat has to do with this, okay? You said you made calls to your big-shot important friends in Washington and they pretended they didn't know you."

"Not quite. They pretended they didn't owe me. There's a difference. So, I have another plan. This one doesn't involve some candy-ass aide-de-rump on Capitol Hill."

"This new plan…it will get me out from under the cops' thumb. I will not have to be killed by the Bratva when they discover I am working for the police. They will, you know. One false step, one muscle guy leaning on one weak man, and I am a dead Cossack."

"You were never a Cossack in your life, Yuri, so forget that. Listen, I can't guarantee anything except that what I have in mind will significantly reduce the chances of you dying before your time and, if I remember my sixth grade geography correctly, might involve some Cossacks after all."

"I am confused. You know that short of miracles, I am going to die? Tell me why I should not get in the van and drive into 'Uncle Bob's' country and disappear?"

"Because Mugabe would put you in the same box. I can't help you in Zimbabwe and I just know that your dying isn't scheduled for today, okay?"

"But you can't tell me when it is or this plan of yours."

"As to the plan, I can. I could. I prefer not to. There are always last minute glitches in any good plan. I needed one or two more phone calls to come through. They did and now we have it."

"We?"

"Exactly. We. You and me and some friends in Chicago and elsewhere. Oh, and add the local police in the person of Kgabo Modise."

"What if he doesn't buy it?"

"There is always that. If he has scruples, we go to plan B."

"You have a plan B?"

"Maybe I do and maybe I don't. Either way he won't know that."

"And you are not going to tell me plan B either, Leo?"

"Nope."

"Why do I feel like I am in a bad television show?"

"Like I said, Yuri, trust me, I have this covered. Oops, here comes our man now."

Painter pointed out the window again. Modise, himself, had stopped to talk to the man mixing cement.

"Brace yourself, Yuri, we are about to play a hand of high stakes Texas no-hold'em."

Chapter Nine

Charles Tlalelo studied his boss behind lidded eyes. What should he say? Would she be angry or have her feelings hurt? He had come to admire this woman who seemed to fear no one and nothing. Sanderson, he'd learned, was not a weak woman, but when it came to those things of the heart, who can tell.

"Charles, you are looking at me like a meerkat looks at an eagle. What is it you have on that mind of yours that has you shaking in your boots?"

"It is nothing, Boss. I am thinking of…I am missing something…my lunch. I forgot to bring my lunch today."

"The box in the fridge with your initials on it is lunch for someone else, then?"

"My initials on a box? Oh, well, yes. I see now. I am mistaken. Yes, I did bring my lunch, Thank you, Sanderson."

"Charles, you will tell me what is eating at your brain right now or I will write a recommendation that you see the doctor because you are definitely going crazy."

"Okay. You are sitting down so, I will say what I must say. Modise, the policeman from Gabz, is here. I saw him going to the American's casino. So there it is."

"Oh yes? And this is of such great importance that you are forgetting your lunch and acting like your undergarments are too tight?"

"Sanderson! No, I thought you and he…I thought he would

have been in touch with you but I heard no phone ringing and so I thought, why is it he doesn't call?"

"Modise will call when he is ready to do so. He is a busy man and if he doesn't call, there will be a reason. I have no claim on that man. We are friends and we sometimes work together. Now, collect your things. We must check out a sick hippopotamus."

"What?"

"One of the river guides calls and says there is a hippo making funny noises down near Sodudu Island. He thinks this hippo is sick. Bring the big tranquilizer gun and loads. We will see what is bothering Mr. Hippo."

"Are you sure you want to do this, Sanderson? Sick or well, those animals are dangerous. One false move and you could add to the statistics of homicide by hippo."

"Charles, it is what we do. Who else do you suggest should go to the river to see about the hippo? Of course I will be extra careful and so will you. Besides, we have not walked the bank for a while. This same river guide reports he thinks he saw evidence of a vehicle having been on the bank. We will check into that as well. *Tsena.*"

"I'm coming, I'm coming."

The only vehicle available was the old Land Rover with the missing doors. How those doors had become detached in the first place, and remained so for so long in the second, had become a source of chronic annoyance for Sanderson. She'd asked, begged, and submitted countless work orders to have the truck repaired and yet, there it stood, still door-less. Some of the younger game rangers preferred this truck. They thought it made them appear rakish and cool when they cruised through Kasane. Sanderson did not have the heart to tell them that the young women they sought to impress with their macho presence, mostly thought they were silly. Her annoyance at the absent doors did not seem to change anything in the one place it could. The doors remained detached. She tried to impress on the repair department the importance doors on a vehicle had. Doors provide a layer of protection from animals with bad attitudes. She'd declared that if doors were not reattached to the truck soon, she would ask her son, Michael, to do the job for her. He could fix anything.

"You hang on tight, Charles, or you will tumble out of the truck when we go around a corner."

"I will have my seat belt. I will be perfectly safe."

"That seat belt is broken as well. It will click and you will be thinking you are tucked in safely but it will unclick with just a tiny tug and out you go. So, we will stay on the main track and away from hungry animals."

They drove into the park and followed a well travelled road that led northward toward the Chobe River. They had gone a kilometer and a half when Sanderson slowed to a crawl.

"Now you must hold onto the handle on the dash very tight, Charles."

"Because?"

"You will see. Hang on."

The front end of the truck jolted and dropped first right and then left. Charles was thrown into Sanderson and then toward the door. He grabbed the dashboard handle and yelped. His seat belt came loose.

Sanderson eyed a frightened Charles Tlalelo "There, you see. That belt is bad."

"What just happened there?"

"Ah, this is for your future education. There is a sharp drop-off at that point in the road. A shallow ridge runs through here for a few hundred meters. You must ease the truck down it or bad things can happen. If you are not careful, you can do some damage to the truck and passengers. Without doors, you might have fallen out, you see."

"Falling out would not be the experience I want."

"It is worse. You see that large area of thirty meters over there? That is one of the places the new lion's pride can sometimes be found. You remember Sekoa? The pride was his. Now there is a new male and things are different. The safari trucks will always look for lions there first."

"They do not drive the tourists over that drop-off, surely."

"No, they turn off the track ten meters or so back and skirt the area from the south. Then when they are finished with the lions, if lions are there, they either turn back or loop around and rejoin the track down twenty-five or so meters farther on."

"Why didn't we take that route? You could have dumped me in the dirt."

"As I said, it is for your education to know about that hazard. Also, this is not the *bakkie* to drive in the park if you can avoid it. With the doors off you are available to the animals and some of them will be hungry for a lunch of Charles. We did not take the detour first, because it is nearly one hundred fifty meters out of our way. Second, today is not the day to tempt a lion. What if they are lolling out there and you have no door to separate you from them? Now you are educated in this very important matter."

If Sanderson had not been grinning, he might have been angry. As it was, Charles smiled back. Sanderson was a good boss no matter what the old-timers said.

They heard yapping and growling and caught the scent of death long before they came upon the hippo. As it happened, determining what ailed the hippopotamus would not be necessary. When they arrived at the riverbank they saw that the vultures and hyenas were having a dispute over which would feast first and most. It wasn't as if there wasn't enough for all, but in the wild there is no concept of sharing and when the topic is food, there is never too much. The strongest would eat until they were sated and then leave the remains for the next highest on the pecking order. Today, spotted hyenas ruled although a daring vulture occasionally darted in and sank its beak into the carcass and managed to escape the combined jaws of the pack. Small scavengers would take what was left and then the ants would clean up. Nothing edible goes to waste in the wild.

They drove west until they found the tire tracks the guide had mentioned.

"What do you think, Sanderson?"

"I cannot say, Charles. These tracks could be from the BDF training for poaching prevention. Of course they usually tell me when they are in the park. The tracks could have been made by smugglers. A man in a coracle poles over from Namibia or maybe has a motor boat upriver from Zambia. He meets his man here at night and off goes the stuff to Gabz to rot the brains of young people."

"I think it does not stop at Gaborone, Boss. There is not enough money there. I think it is on its way to Jo'berg. Many more brains to rot and money to pay for the privilege in that town."

"I hope you are right, but I am thinking they are connected to our latest visitors to Kasane. They are not so nice people, these newcomers. That woman, they say, is a big problem."

"Is that what Modise the policeman says to you?"

"No. He thinks like a man. He thinks the problem is Rra Lenka. But I think it is his woman."

"Do you know the woman who is with the crook?"

"I have observed this woman one time when she insisted the hotel take her and her man only into the park for safari. She was very bossy and the man, he just smiled a weak smile. She is the alpha in that group for sure."

"All this you assume from that one meeting?"

"It was enough. You will see."

"I hope I will never see, if you want the truth."

"With any luck, you will not. Now, take pictures of those tracks and we will report them to Superintendent Mwambe."

"Are you sure he is the person you wish to have this information? He is not exactly your great fan."

"He is the police. It is his job to stop smugglers. He will receive the report. Now we must get back and write up the dead hippo and send pictures to Mwambe."

"Can we avoid that tooth-cracking hazard on the way back? Perhaps we should check and see if the lions are in the bush over there."

"You have not been listening, Charles. Besides, you have seen the lions many times, Charles. We have work to do, so, no. We take the bump. It will not be so bad coming at it from this side. You will see."

Chapter Ten

Leo and Yuri watched Modise cross the ten meters between them and the door. Modise knocked and entered without waiting for a response.

"Police Officer Kgabo Modise, come in. Oh, you're in already. So, to what do we owe the honor?" Leo said.

"I am here to speak to Mr. Greshenko. Could I have a word?"

Leo was not to be put off. "Certainly, shoot."

"I wish to address Mr. Greshenko alone."

"We have no secrets."

"Nevertheless, I must insist. I wish to speak to him in private."

"Not happening, Modise. My house, my rules. You are here to complete the subornation of my friend. I am here to prevent you from getting him killed. You can have your little talk, but as this is, as I said, my house I have no intention of leaving. Can I order you something? A beer, coffee…?"

"No drinks, thank you."

Yuri slumped in his chair. "It's okay, Inspector. Leo knows everything. He is only here to help."

"This is police work. With respect for his acknowledged skill in the world of business, I cannot see where any help will be coming from your employer."

"Hey, I'm over here, right? I can hear you and besides, I'm not just his employer. I am his friend and as such, I will stay."

"Very well, if you insist, but I must warn you, nothing said here can be shared with anyone else."

Leo waved in the direction of the window. "Including your flunky out there?"

"Why do you think that man is 'my flunky' as you say?"

"It's kind of obvious, don't you think? You just had a short chat with him. Also, he's got cop written all over him. Really, Modise, if I can spot someone who is not what he seems, don't you suppose the crooks you're after can too? After all, they have had much more practice at that sort of thing than I."

"That's enough, Leo," Yuri cut in. "Tell me what you want, Modise. Mr. Painter may not like it, but he will not tell anyone about it."

"Very well. As you know, your continued presence in the country is contingent on your cooperation in our investigation of this Russian Bratva operative, Oleg Lenka. We are in agreement on that point?"

"As you tell me repeatedly, you have discovered my past, yes, and you think I am an undesirable and cannot stay in your country. The past, by the way, which I had hoped to put behind me forever. You have found me out. This man Lenka has a similar past but you allow him to stay. How that is possible is a question I guess you'd rather not answer."

"It is ironic, but he has no 'official' past. That is, there are no warrants for his arrest on record anywhere. Were there, we would not be having this meeting because neither of you would be here. So, you see, we cannot send him away but we can send you. The moment he does something, we will send him packing. That is where you come in."

Leo sat down. His chair was new and the cushion sighed as it took his weight. "You realize that what you are doing is one, extortion and, two, a near certain death sentence for Yuri? The first is a felony crime in most countries and the second would be considered accessory to murder."

"Mr. Painter, you may listen, but you are not invited to speak."

"Nevertheless."

Yuri waved Leo into silence "Just tell me what you want me to do, Modise. Whether I die here or in Russia makes no difference to me, I will still be dead."

"I hope not, but very well. We want you to become Lenka's man. He will tell you things. You will tell us what he says. That is all."

"I am a double agent, is that what you see?"

"Yes. Then as soon as we gather enough information, we will eliminate his organization forever."

Leo stared to say something and thought better of it. Yuri lowered his head and shook it. "I am a dead man."

"Not if you are careful, surely."

"Modise, how much do you really know about these criminal organizations that hover over your country like…what is your word…*manong*?"

"I have studied them, read extensively. We have analyses from Interpol, the American FBI. Quite a bit, I should think."

"Then you know little or nothing. Lenka will have as many spies in place as you do. If he doesn't already know we are talking right now, he soon will. You have your man outside. Don't you suppose he also has one? My becoming an operative for you, he will know already or soon. If I am to survive for more than a minute in this, I will have to tell him up front that I am your agent and that he can use me to spread false news to you, you see?"

Modise leaned back and seemed confused. "This is not what I have been asked to do."

"Okay, I've heard enough," Leo said. "You will spend, what, two hundred thousand pula each to airlift rhinoceroses into the Okavango but, you will throw this rhino, this man, to the poachers in the hope of catching a scrap of information. You care more about your damned animals than people. You should be ashamed, Modise."

"Mr. Painter, I must insist. This is police business and of no concern of yours."

"Ah, but it is. Here's what I think. You have the wrong end of the stick and you will get nowhere with this cockamamie plan. Now, I'll tell you what you need to do instead."

"Mr. Painter, you really must—"

"Just sit and listen. My house, my rules, remember?" Leo stuck two fingers into his bush vest and withdrew a Cuban cigar. He lit it and inspected both ends. Satisfied, he sat back. "Docs told me these will kill me. I told them there are worse ways to die." He drew in and exhaled a plume of smoke. "Okay. If Yuri does as you ask, not what he suggested, by the way, he will not last six hours. Whether he passes the information on to you directly or through some intermediary, Lenka will know. Then, Yuri will disappear. As Yuri just pointed out, there is a better than even chance, a certainty I would venture to say, that they know you are meeting with him right now. You are not the only person who knows Yuri's background. Lenka has used him once before. You don't think he has eyes on him now? Ask yourself this, what is it that Lenka wants?"

"To introduce crime and corruption into the Chobe."

"That's only a C+ answer. You can do better. You've just scratched the surface. What does he want, Yuri?"

Yuri frowned at Leo and shook his head. "First, Lenka wants this casino. Next, he wants to take it over and then sell protection to the other hotels, introduce working girls, and skim profits, control the liquor trade—"

"And that's just the start, Modise. He would like to control this section of the border, black market, you name it, he would like to own it. To start, he will use Yuri to eliminate me, don't you see? Somehow, someway, he wants this casino. It is the springboard into the rest."

"But how can he do that?"

"Muscle, strong arm, force me to sign over control to Yuri or to him and then I disappear, and it doesn't end there. You will be next. Most Russian gangs work with corrupt police. They promise to reduce petty crime and in return only ask you turn a blind eye to what they are doing in the dark. See, if you buy that, you will be allowed to arrest the bit players, a drug dealer, a small smuggler, a prostitute. It will appear you are doing your job but, for some reason, you never get the big fish. They think this arrangement is a win-win. Are you prepared for that? If you aren't, and they are established here as a base, you will join Yuri among the casualties."

Modise slumped down in his chair. "So you are suggesting the operation is finished before it starts?"

"Your version of it, yes. Sorry, but I don't think you've thought it through. Somewhere in one of those books you read you figured out a plan. What was it called, 'How to infiltrate the mob?' It's not good enough. They read the same books, you could say. You need to try something off the books. What do the motivational speakers say? 'You must think outside the box.' Modise, think outside the box."

Modise rose to leave. Leo's words must have had an effect. "This will not do."

"Sit. I am not finished. First, how do you suppose Lenka will react when he discovers someone got to me first?"

"Someone beat him to taking over your casino?"

"Right,"

"But who? How?"

"Okay, you know I used to run a company called Earth Global. We specialized in energy resources, among other things. As you probably also know, things in the Ukraine are somewhat dicey at the moment and Gazprom is in hot water with the EU. No? Not a hot item on the evening news? Never mind. The point is, there are a half dozen Earth Global employees sitting at desks in Chicago with nothing to do at the moment. More importantly, they speak Russian with a Ukrainian accent. That's what I have been told, anyway. Three of them are ex-Army Spec Forces."

Modise started to speak and then thought better of it. Greshenko frowned.

Leo placed his cigar in an ashtray. "So here's the deal. The six of them are, at this moment on a plane to Cape Town. They will arrive here sometime late tomorrow or the next day. They will be Yuri's alternate to Lenka."

"What?" Greshenko and Modise said in unison.

"Yuri, when you ran an errand for Lenka last month, would you say you behaved in a manner consistent with someone as interested in gathering information as someone just caving in to threats?"

Yuri thought a moment and shook his head and then his eyes flashed. "Ah! Okay, but what about the tattoos?"

"Tattoos?" Modise was clearly out of the loop. "What tattoos…why?"

"There are fakes we can use if we need them. They will last long enough to convince Lenka's people our guys are the real thing."

For the first time in months Yuri's eyes showed a hint of optimism. "It might work. It's better than committing suicide. What do you think, Modise?"

"About what? I am lost. Who has tattoos?"

"Bratva *apparatchiks* do. They mark their journey into the depths of crime. Where they've been in prison, things like that. I'll explain later. We will need guns and fake IDs. Can you arrange that?

"IDs and guns, and an alternate to…Sorry, I need this spelled out to me. I am a simple policeman, remember?"

"You are many things, I think, but simple isn't one of them. Look, you are limited in what you can do, in resources you can call in. I, on the other hand, have access to all sorts of things not generally available to the average citizen. We will assemble a rival Bratva gang that will challenge Lenka. Given the new circumstances this will create he will be much more likely to do something truly felonious or stupid. Either will work for us."

"Oh, I see. Yuri will be competition and draw them out. Yes?"

"And I will be the idiotic American who brought this on himself, yes. In a nutshell, yes. It will be a little more complex than that, but that is where you start. So far, if I understand the situation, Lenka has been tidying up—removing local crooks and an occasional interloper from outside. He has no real competition in the area now. Another Bratva group is a different kettle of fish. The threat of a war between competing gangs will identify the players quickly. You pick them off as they emerge from the woodwork. He will understand that the Chobe is not his for the taking. He will have to rethink his plans. If we are lucky, he will be slow to figure it all out."

"I am not familiar with woodwork, but I think I follow. So, now it is you who airlifts the *ditshukudu*, sorry, the rhinos, into the park. At what expense? Never mind, I do not want to know. I will notify my boss of the change. When he understands, he will be pleased. I hope."

"And if he isn't?"

"Well, you have a saying, I think. 'Sometimes it is better to ask for forgiveness than permission.' Yes?"

"Yes."

Chapter Eleven

Irena Davidova sat in the passenger side of the HiLux and scanned the casino as Lenka drove by. He was talking about gaming and how free liquor always paid for itself when you gave it to gamblers because they became reckless and lost much more money. He said it had to be cheap whiskey or vodka, but there was no shortage of that. Irena listened with half an ear. Her mind was on the building and how she would have Oleg build her a penthouse on top. Well, it wouldn't be much of a penthouse, really. The casino had only three floors. Still, she could have something like a fourth story added overlooking the pool and café seating around it. That would be something. A long balcony with a view of the bush, too. She decided she would like living in the wild and dangerous country with its lions and gorillas. Were there gorillas in Botswana? She'd have to ask. If there were none, maybe they could buy one and have it in a big cage behind the hotel. That would be a draw, wouldn't it? Yes, she needed a safe place to settle. No more St. Petersburg ice and snow. No more freezing in the winter for Irena.

"You are not listening to me, Irena."

"Yes I am. You were speaking of the whiskey."

"That was ten minutes ago. I asked you if you were hungry and you said 'We need a gorilla.' What is that all about? There are no gorillas in Botswana, only baboons and monkeys."

At that moment a gray monkey dashed across the road. Lenka braked and swerved to avoid hitting it. Irena could have sworn the monkey grinned at her as if to say something naughty.

"You must catch that monkey, Oleg. I want him."

"Catch him? He's gone. You will not see that fellow again for a long time. If he keeps dancing in front of automobiles, he will not last long, either."

"You will get me a monkey?"

"I already told you. You cannot collect or hunt the animals here. One of the Boers we hired tells me they shoot poachers in this country. How would it look if we come all this way and end up shot to death by the local army for poaching? Anyway, I thought you said gorilla. I will get you neither one. Come, we will be late for our meeting."

Sanderson saw the *bakkie* nearly hit the monkey and braked to make sure it managed to avoid disaster. She watched as it raced across the grassy lawn in front of the casino and disappeared into the trees beyond. She also noticed the people in the truck. It was that Russian who troubled Kgabo Modise so much, and his woman. She had to admit that the woman was very pretty but at the same time she looked like she might have been carved from stone. A hard woman was that one, for sure. Sanderson reengaged the gears and drove on. The Russian woman's face stuck in her mind. What was it about the woman that reminded her of something or someone else? She couldn't think what. It would come to her later. At this moment she contemplated the ways she might help her friend Modise bring this woman and her man down. He should use her and her cadre of game rangers to end this business. Bodies in the park was a very bad thing for the animals.

Leo and Yuri allowed Modise to take over the desk in the corner to make his calls. This new plan needed the okay from the boss. Also, he needed to catch up with Sanderson. He tried her number first and spoke to Charles Tlalelo who told him she was out. Should she call back? Modise said he'd try later. His boss put him on hold for five minutes and then they spoke. It would take another twenty minutes and an occasional side conversation with Leo Painter before he received the go-ahead he needed. The operation was on. What to call it?

Greshenko stared at Leo for a minute. He shook his head. "You had this all worked out weeks ago, didn't you?"

"I confess, I had a thought."

"But you didn't share."

"No."

"Why is that?"

"Why? Okay here's the thing. If I work this out in the open, it wouldn't stay a secret past lunch. This place is porous to information. I don't know if it is jungle drums or what, but secrets are as rare as hen's teeth out here. Lenka has to believe the guys who will arrive soon enough are, in fact, a rival Bratva from the States and are here to shove him out of the Chobe. Besides, there was always the chance the Government would change its mind and leave you alone. It was a long chance, I admit, but worth taking. At any rate, I was willing to wait on both counts."

"Do you think Modise's boss will buy it?"

"He'd better. Anything else is going to fail before it starts and either way be a bloody mess."

"And it will be my blood that is making the mess."

"Possibly. On the other hand, it is equally possible you will disappear from the face of the earth. The bad news would be at the hands of the Bratva or the Botswana government. The good news, with the offices of some people I know, and the right amount of cash, that might also happen. You disappear, I mean, not die."

"Why don't we just do that bit right now and forget Lenka and the Batswana."

"We could, but then I would be dead and the Russians would own my hotel and I am not willing to allow that to happen. I am settled here. I like this place and I won't admit it to him, but I kind of like Modise."

Modise, as if he heard the last comment, shouted across the room, "We are calling it 'Moscow Nights.' What do you think?"

"I think it sounds like someone reads too many cheap thrillers. Also, I think that clown is from St. Petersburg, not Moscow. By the way, Inspector Modise, when you leave, look angry, like your interview with Yuri went badly. They will know by now that you were here and will want to hear what happened. They should think Yuri stiffed you. Yuri, you can expect to be contacted by that freaking sewer rat any time now. Okay, we're in business."

Chapter Twelve

Since her son Michael had rallied from what Sanderson believed to have been certain death, she made it a point to keep in touch with him every day. It had been easy enough when he had lived at home but, since his AIDs symptoms had disappeared and his health had returned to near normal, he had returned to his small apartment over the garage where he worked. Sanderson accepted the move but, did not like it. Recovering HIV patients relapsed, didn't they? Shouldn't they stay at home with their mothers? She thanked *Modimo* every day for this miracle and worried anyway. What if there had been no miracle and he relapsed?

She parked the door-less Land Rover on the gravel lot and poked her head in the garage. The men who were working on automobiles smiled and greeted her. She could hardly make herself heard over the din caused by the panel beaters hammering and grinding. No, they shouted, Michael had not arrived at work today. No, they did not think he was sick. When they said this, one or two of them grinned. Sanderson wondered at that.

She thanked them and rounded the building corner to climb the stairs to Michael's flat. She tried the door handle. Locked? She knocked. No answer. Now, she had a reason to worry. His friends said he was not sick but, how would they know? Would he tell them if he was? Maybe he was lying in bed feverish and sweating with his disease back again? She remembered that all too well, this fading away disease. Should she call the ambulance service? She pounded on the door.

Something or someone stirred inside. The door opened a few centimeters. Two eyes peered out. Not Michael's eyes.

"Yes? Who is it?"

"Is Michael home? Is he all right?" Who belonged to these eyes?

"You are Mma Michael." Not a question.

"Yes, what has happened?" The eyes disappeared.

"Michael, it is your momma."

The door clicked shut. What is this? The door is closed on me? Sanderson knocked again. Michael's voice, muffled by the closed door. "I am here, Ma. Coming." The door swung open again, all the way.

"Michael, are you ill? The men downstairs are saying you did not come to work today." Sanderson lifted herself up on tiptoes and tried to peek into the room behind her son.

Michael smiled and stepped aside to let her in. "Sorry, come in."

It took a moment for her eyes to adjust to the gloom. Michael had the blinds drawn. Why do this in the middle of the day? Then she saw the girl, the young woman, the owner of the eyes at the door earlier.

"Ma, this is Sekgele Andersen. You know her father."

"You are the daughter of the Hyena Man. Yes, I see." Did she? The girl nodded and dropped her gaze to the floor.

"So, Michael…?"

"Sekgele and I, we are—"

"I think I am old enough to see what you two are about, Michael. But, are you well enough and…can you be safe with this girl?"

In a country which struggled with AIDS, the whole area of human sexuality and relationships had acquired an entirely different focus than in most other places.

"We are protected, if that is what you are asking, and before you go there, no, her father does not know."

"He must be told, Michael. He has a right to know."

"He will not allow it because of the AIDS, Ma. Sekgele and I, we are in love and this is what we must do."

"No, I am sorry, Michael, but this is not what you must do. You must be honest with Sekgele's father. He is a respectable man and has the right to know. He raised you by himself, Sekgele. It could not have been an easy thing for him. If the situation were reversed, I would want to know."

"We can talk of this later. Are you to visit or to play momma with me?"

"You be careful how you say that, Mister. You may be a big man now but, I was the one who changed your nappies. You can repair an engine but, I taught you how to use a spoon."

"Yes, Ma. Sorry. What else can I do?"

"So, okay, I came to ask a favor. I am driving one of our older Game Ranger vehicles. It has lost its doors. They came loose and were removed for fear they would drop off while the truck was moving and be broken past fixing. I have put in many work orders and nothing has happened. It is parked downstairs. Can you help me and replace the doors on the truck?"

"Ah. So, here is what we will do. I do you a favor and you do me one. I will fix this truck and you will allow me to inform Rra Andersen in my own way and time. Okay?"

Sanderson shook her head and looked at the girl. She was very pretty and, downcast eyes or not, she looked like she had her share of brains. Sanderson realized this must be something that Michael and the girl had to work out on their own. She turned to Michael, considered her answer. Her heart said no, her brain said yes. "Okay, then, but you must promise to do what you know you must do and soon."

"I will."

"So, the grinning I received from those panel beaters downstairs was about you and…I see. Are you not missed?"

"I am assigned engines fulltime now, Ma. I am moving up in the world."

"You are being silly."

"No, no, it is true. These cars coming here from Japan have sophisticated computer systems. I have taken the course and now I am the man they turn to on the newer models. Also, I am paid more. Soon, I will have enough to buy a little house and leave this noisy flat."

"Is this true? I am proud of you Michael, but…" Sanderson didn't quite know how to say or what came next. How long would this relation last if the disease returned? Was this pretty girl up to nursing a sick man? Had Sanderson been? Well, not at first, but she had adapted and she learned. Sekgele had strength, she knew, but enough?

"The 'but' you are struggling to say is, I don't know. I feel fine. HAART is working. I am not unusual in this, Ma. Many of us with HIV are growing stronger. We have limitations with some of the things, make that many things we can do, but the future looks pretty good to me."

"But…?"

"Another 'but,' yes. Okay, I am sorry, Ma. I will be a wonderful uncle. But, you must look to Mpitle if you want grandchildren. I know this is not what you want, but it is the facts, no matter what I do. Sekgele knows this and is okay with it."

"I read where there are ways to…maybe as low as two percent of the babies are—"

"It is not something they can do here, Ma, and unless it was zero percent, I would not do it. It would mean that Sekgele…I would not wish this disease on anyone."

"No, of course not." Sanderson's heart ached. "Very well, Michael. Call me when you can do the repairs. Oh, I am so sorry, Sekgele, I did not introduce myself properly. How do you do? Now that was awkward. I am happy for you and Michael. I am the mother and it is the way we operate sometimes. You will please forgive me for seeming rude. I didn't mean to be. It is just—"

"I understand, Mma Michael."

Sanderson smiled. "Yes, you do. I can see that. So, you will tell me if there is any…well, you know."

The girl looked up and her face lit up with a grin that could melt anyone's heart. "I will Mma Michael," she said and rushed over and hugged Sanderson. "I love him, Ma."

"Go on you two. Listen, you both will come Sunday for dinner, yes? I will ask my friend Modise to join us and you can tell me everything. Now, I think I am in the way of some unfinished business."

Sanderson went back down the stairs and to her truck. She had to admit that Michael seemed healthy, and happy. That Sekgele seemed a nice girl and also seemed happy. All that got Sanderson to worrying. Mothers are only happy when they worry about their children.

Chapter Thirteen

The Air Botswana BAe 146, blue and white paint gleaming, touched down in Kasane late in the afternoon. Greshenko stood in the baking noonday sun next to the casino van and waited. In spite of the heat, he wore a black suit, shirt, and tie. The differences in the fabrics of each caused the light to reflect variously, creating the effect of three shades of black, were such a thing possible. He'd told Leo he looked like Hollywood's idea of a mobster. Leo said that was the whole idea. His appearance should attract attention, which was the point. It would make it easy for his new playmates to find him and for Modise to keep track. Yuri groused a bit and said something that sounded obscene or it may have been Russian, probably both. The sun seemed particularly unrelenting and the reek of kerosene made him queasy. He exhaled, pulled out a handkerchief and mopped his face. He felt the presence of others, like himself, who were not there to greet passengers, but to watch. Lenka would have his people in the small crowd of greeters. So would Modise. The presence of the latter was supposed to make him feel safe. It didn't.

The Bratva boss had not taken it well when Greshenko told him the police had questioned him. He already knew that, of course, but wanted to know what they were after and what, if anything, they already knew. Yuri had told him they were aware of Lenka's plans to muscle in on the Chobe hotels, but didn't know the details. But then, anybody who had been paying attention to what had been going on for the last month or so could have figured that much out. He'd added that the police did not know about his own plans, either. Yuri felt sure that remark had thrown Lenka off stride. So, he had plowed on and added, almost as an afterthought, he would not be interested in anything Lenka had to say as he had business of his own to attend to. There'd been a short silence and the line went dead. Lenka would wonder about the reasons why Yuri Greshenko, whom he thought to be his to do with as he pleased, had become so independent. How did that happen? Yuri was sure he would not take the snub lightly but, if he knew anything, he knew how a Bratva mind worked and he knew Lenka would wait and see what it was that had emboldened the person he'd believed was under his thumb to defy him before he moved against him.

Yuri pulled out a dry handkerchief (not black) and mopped his brow again. It wasn't as much a matter of nerves as leaving his back unguarded. He might have missed something about Lenka and if he had, he could expect to hear the pop of a silenced pistol and feel the shock of a bullet at any moment. It would not be a new experience and certainly one he did not wish to repeat. He put that thought aside and turned his attention to the passengers alighting from the plane.

A mixture of a few business types and many tourists dressed in what they must have assumed to be proper safari wear stepped onto the tarmac and made their way to the vans marked with hotel names on their doors. Six men, all in their late thirties or early forties, peeled off from the crowd and walked toward Yuri. They waved and smiled as if they were meeting an old friend, a colleague. In truth, none of them had ever laid eyes on Yuri except for the photographs Leo had sent them by e-mail with instructions about how they were to behave when they arrived. As they drew nearer, they greeted Yuri in Russian and piled into the van while making as much noise within the bounds of normal as they could. Yuri drove them to the casino.

The game was on.

〉〉〉

Sanderson had to stop at the airport. A package delivery had arrived and one which required her urgent attention, Charles Tlalelo had said. She knew Charles always exaggerated, but she didn't want to take a chance and miss something important. He also told her that her policeman had called and would try to reach her later. She was sorry she'd missed that call. She started to call Modise and then changed her mind. That must be for another time. She was on duty and had to adhere to stricter standards than the others. It was the price she paid for being a woman in a man's job. That is how it was put to her. Progress was slow coming to the Chobe, for sure. The package turned out to be new patches for the Game Park Guides uniforms and surely not the hurry-up job Charles imagined, but she did catch sight of Kgabo Modise. He seemed preoccupied with watching a man in a black suit who was busy greeting six suspicious-looking men. They seemed very friendly and after much backslapping, they drove off in the new casino's van. Modise remained in place until they were out of sight and then made a call on his mobile. He started to walk toward a car Sanderson recognized as belonging to the Army. The Army? Modise is working with them? She caught his eye and waved. He smiled and changed course so that their paths would cross.

"So, Kgabo Modise, you are here to see the planes and their passengers or is it official business, then?"

"Some of the passengers are of official interest, you could say, yes, and one or two of those who come to greet them."

"The man in the silly black suit of clothes, isn't that the Russian who works for the American at the casino?

"It is. He is a person of interest to me."

"Oh, yes? In that case, I will not disturb you in your duties." She turned to leave.

"You are leaving? Wait, I have done what I came to do at this place. It is hot, don't you think?"

"Sorry? Hot? It is the Chobe, Modise. Unless it rains, which is almost never, it is always hot here."

"Yes, of course. I was thinking that perhaps, if you have time, a cold drink might be a nice thing to have about now."

"Oh, you are speaking of that sort of hot. So, you have a place in mind where this cold drink might be found?"

"This is the place where the romantic hero says, 'Your place or mine?' and they go off together."

"My place is a rondeval with a tin roof and a not-so-big extension. It is definitely not available. So?"

"And mine is a government building I share with others."

"You are not at a hotel this time?"

"No. The government is economizing. We have a rented house in Kasane now."

"The restaurant at the Mowana. It is the closest."

"As I said, economizing, and it would be best if I am not so obvious a person in the area just now. For sure, I do not think I should hang around that particular hotel. Perhaps I can visit a bottle shop and they will supply us with ice and something appropriate for midday, and you can show me the park. I wish to see it as you do, not as a tourist."

"You will need some very good luck to find ice, Modise, but the park is the place for privacy, for sure, just you, me, and a thousand elephants."

"You are being so romantic."

"We must all economize, it seems. There is a place down by the river which in the afternoon will have a breeze and fewer mosquitoes than anywhere else I know. We will slather ourselves with repellant and have our sundowner, only it will be at noon."

"And hot."

"And no ice."

"Yes."

"Isn't there a little bar attached to the Chobe Game Lodge that looks out on Sududu Island that serves drinks?"

"There is, and I know the place. Do you suppose they are open in the afternoon?"

"We will find that out."

◇◇◇

Lenka's man drove to the Mowana Lodge and rang his boss. They met outside. Lenka kept his local people separate from his public appearances.

"What have you got for me, Kindo?"

"The Greshenko person met six other men at the airport. They all spoke in Russian."

"You're sure it was Russian?"

Kindo scratched his head and cocked an eyebrow over his good eye. "I think so. I do not know Russian, but I do know it was not English. I do not think it was French or Spanish. I have heard those people speak and it did not sound like that. They sounded like you when you speak to the old lady."

"The what?"

"Your woman."

"Why did you call her the 'old lady'?"

"Oh, so sorry. It is how we speak of the men's women. It is a term of respect, Rra Lenka."

"Well, I don't like it. You will call her Mma Davidova from now on. 'Mma' is what you say, am I correct?"

"Yes, sir, we do most of the time. Some European ladies do not like that any better than the 'old lady.' They want us to say Missus."

"Well, you call her Mma Davidova unless I tell you otherwise. Tell me about the men Greshenko met. What did they look like?"

"Um…They looked like you."

"Me? They looked like me? How did they look like me?

"They were white, tall, and…um…"

"What?"

"Mean."

"Ah. I guess Greshenko is not what he said he was. He is not just here hoping to escape a life in the gangs. He lied. He must have an organization of his own. He was feeling me out. So, not so stupid, that one."

"Sir?"

"Never mind. See Cszepanski about your pay and stay in touch. I may need you again soon. Do you know how to fire a gun?"

"Oh, yes, I can do that."

"Good, then you can stick around."

Chapter Fourteen

As it happened, the bar was closed and, as predicted, the bottle store had no ice. The clerk suggested they go to one of the hotels if they wanted their drinks chilled. In the end Sanderson and Modise bought a few cold beers and drove into the park. Sanderson took the river road. After bouncing along the road for a quarter of an hour, Sanderson turned west which put them onto a smaller and less defined track. It took them away from the river road.

"We have left the track, Sanderson. We are not going to the river now?"

"Later, yes, but first, a treat for you. I am taking you to see the lions."

"Lions? I have seen lions before, Sanderson. Is there something special about these particular lions that I must see?"

"In my eyes there is and you said you wished to see my park as I see it, yes? So, we will visit the lions. We will, that is, if they are there today. Sometimes in the afternoon they move closer to the river where it is cooler, but most of the time we will find them here. Ah, there, you see? The safari trucks from the lodges have found them and are already parked. That means the lions are waiting for us."

They drove slowly past the three safari trucks and edged closer to a clearing in the dry brush. A lone acacia tree provided a measure of shade for the pride. Some preferred to bask in the sun. They were a magnificent sight. Modise had seen lions before.

He was Motswana. Of course he had seen lions, but he had to admit that he'd never been this close or witnessed anything quite so magnificent. The animals stretched out, some sleeping, some watching the tourist vehicles as if they were hoping a fat tourist would hop out and provide them with lunch. He could almost hear them purring like big pussy cats. They weren't, but he imagined they were.

"So, what does the city policeman think of my lions?"

"Your lions? You have purchased this pride?"

"It is a figure of speech, silly. Of course not. Oh, you are making a joke."

"A poor one, I am afraid. Sanderson, I admit, they are most impressive. But I worry about our time and our bottles of beer. If we don't find the riverbank soon, our drinks will be warm and not so good."

Sanderson put the truck in gear and kept moving westward as they circled around the pride.

Modise swiveled in his seat and looked back at the way they had come. "We are not going to the river?"

"We are. This way brings us back out on the road farther down and nearer the river. It will save us time."

As they approached the river, the growth became more forest and less bush. Also the humidity climbed. At the river she reversed, made a three-point turn, and parked. After checking for wildlife, they climbed out and moved to the back of the truck.

In front of them, the river flowed eastward toward the Zambezi. They sat on the tailgate, rifle close at hand. There was no real danger this close to the river, but caution dictated the gun. It would be too great a distance for a crocodile to heave itself across the riverbank and come after them, and they reckoned there would be no threat from the hippos in the heat of the afternoon. These deceivingly fast giants preferred the water to land, though they had been known to attack an unwary tourist who wandered too close to their territory on the bank or in a boat. A small herd of gazelles had scattered when they drove up.

Now, in the relative quiet, the delicate animals began to drift back to drink and graze in the shade.

Sanderson uncapped two bottles and handed one to Modise. "So, can you speak of the operation you are running in the area? Will you catch this bad man, this Lenka, and put him away forever?"

"About the plans, I cannot, sorry. As to Lenka, it is not so easy. He is a man who is like a snake in the water. He slithers away from you and disappears. You never know where he will pop up. He has no outstanding warrants out, even though Interpol has a watch on him. His crimes to date are all in Russia and it seems like their police system is for sale to the highest bidder. At least for the Bratva it is. So, we must wait until he does something against the law here. Our hope is that he will make a big mistake so that we can deport him back home with all of his people. Then, we round up the locals. The border crossers we send home, the rest visit our jails."

Sanderson sipped her beer. It was not a drink she really enjoyed. It tasted bitter and fizzy. Not a combination that suited her. Although, on some very hot days and after she had been in the field many hours, a very cold beer was welcome. That was not the case now. Keeping company with Kgabo Modise, however, did make it almost enjoyable.

"I would think that he would be considered an undesirable person and his visa cancelled. Why is he still here?"

"It is not so simple, that. The thinking is that if he were expelled, someone as bad, maybe worse would just take his place. Also, we are under the impression that he is not the real brains of the operation and the person who is, has a clean slate."

"Who is this brain?"

"The woman with him is, they say. Her name is Irena Davidova. She no warrants, no real reason to deny her a visitor's visa."

"Oh. So, now you agree with me about the woman?"

"I don't know for sure, but she is now my prime interest. Okay, I say that but it is still the man we want. He pays the bills, you could say. We get him, we get her, we get them all."

"So, will he do something illegal? Or will she?"

"It doesn't matter who or which. The orders come from him and I am certain eventually he will be the one who acts. I am equally certain he already has. The dead policeman didn't just happen because Rra Botlhokwa had disagreements with his organization. The problem is, I can't prove it. We will get him sooner or later, for sure."

"Sooner would be better. What can the game rangers do to help?"

Modise cocked an eyebrow. "You are joking."

"I am not. We know the area better than you do, you people who come up here from Gaborone in your suits. Even Superintendent Mwambe knows more about this place than you. We are the ones who found your bones, remember, and they are important, yes?"

"Yes. That is true, but—"

Sanderson slumped forward and scowled, jaw set. "You are too filled up with 'buts,' Modise. We have to be considered in this business. Why do you think I showed you the lions?"

"So that I could see the Chobe as you do, you said. Very impressive they were."

"I showed them to you to remind you that we are not afraid of danger. What do you think would happen if one of those animals went rogue? I will tell you. Some of us would have to go out and confront it just like you confront your Russian gangster."

"Yes, I understand but—"

"Buts again. Suppose this man continues to dump his dead bodies in the park. Who will be tasked to take care of that? My people will be, that is who. So there, we are important. Who found that wallet of the man they tell me is your dead agent, even though Mwambe and his slow nephew are now upset about it? I did. If I had not done that, where would your investigation be? Do you know Derek Kgasa, the nephew, is now permanently assigned to us? He is underfoot all the time. I am surprised he isn't sitting in the backseat taking notes and drinking our beer."

"There, you see. You have mentioned the man who thinks you should be removed completely. Superintendent Mwambe is complaining about you and your people, but mostly about you, all of the time. 'You meddle where you are not welcome,' he says. He is not happy with you, Sanderson."

"He is a man past his time of usefulness. He should be retired and put to work feeding the chickens."

Modise brushed away a mosquito. "You are being very hard on him. I have seen him work a crime scene. He is very thorough when he puts his mind to it. Besides that is not a decision you will be asked to make."

Sanderson rolled her eyes and snorted. "Which is not the big news of the day. Besides, what has he to do with solving your problem? You are not taking him into your confidence, are you?" Modise stared at the river and said nothing. "I thought not. So, why not me and the game rangers?"

Alerted by movement in the brush, the gazelles bounded away. A few spotted hyenas came panting to the river to drink. They inspected Modise and Sanderson much as the lions had earlier. Sanderson saw them and instinctively put a protective hand on Modise's arm. Modise shook his head. He might have been suppressing a smile; Sanderson could not be sure. "It is not in your description of duties. As you just pointed out, you manage many dangerous beings, lions and leopards, and those hyenas who sit and stare at us over there, but criminals are not supposed to be one of them."

"The big hyena is Kotsi Mosadi. If you think your criminals are bad news, you should spend an afternoon with that one. She and that pack of hers are wondering if they dare make a dash at us. They would love to have a policeman for their dinner. And, yes, we deal with bad things like them all the time, you know. Also, don't forget, we are the only people in this area who are permitted to have rifles and to fire them. We know the ground and its dangers. We are out and about all the time and see things you do not. Why not use us?"

Modise turned and gave her his most serious policeman's look. "There is the other thing. It was one of your people who arranged for the break through the fence and the nonsense in the park with the orgonite, which cost a young man his life and started a series of events that ended with a dead policeman. There is some evidence one of them still does, or how else do these gangsters bring the bodies to the park? The director has not forgotten the first and worries about the second. So, for now, no game rangers will be placed in the loop."

"One bad egg…there is another one betraying his trust?"

"Do not concern yourself with that. We want him in place for the time being. If we arrest him, Lenka will only find another or make different arrangements. Worse, he will know that we know."

"That makes sense only to a policeman. He is breaking the law, deceiving his co-workers, and giving a bad name to my department."

"Sorry, Sanderson, that is the way it must be. You must attend to your animals and the safety of the tourists. Police work will be done by police, not civilians. Later, if the circumstances change, we might talk again about the game rangers, but not now."

When he said it, Modise knew that it wasn't entirely true. He would be relying heavily on a civilian with a criminal record, six Americans with more energy than skill, and the aging owner of a casino, to set in motion the circumstances that would bring down Lenka. And he didn't like it at all. Greshenko might be the reformed man he claimed, but do leopards change their spots? Do hyenas eat vegetables?

Chapter Fifteen

Lenka paced. Twelve steps out, twelve back. Irena sipped a vodka martini and waited. It would be only a matter of time before he would ask her what to do. He wouldn't put it quite like that. He would ask her what she thought about the Greshenko person. Then, instead of answering the question he'd expect her to lay out what needed to be done. He pivoted and returned to the middle of the room.

"So, what do you think we should do with Greshenko, Renee?"

"I think he needs to disappear before he gets his people in place. Maybe four or five of you could just reduce his organization to a memory."

"So, I should…?"

"Eliminate them. Find a way to lure them away from the casino, and introduce them to the game park. If they are deep enough in and, say, unable to run, well, nature has a way of cleaning up messes, yes?"

"I don't know. Since we have been using their park for clean-up, the police are watching everything I do more closely than ever."

"If the police are honest about it, they will say you are doing them a service. Just don't get caught."

"Don't get caught? What kind of an answer is that? I need a plan with some details. I cannot just keep picking up people who get in the way and dropping them off for the lions."

"No? Why not? Okay, you need a plan. Yes, of course you do. Can you think of a plan, then?"

"How does a person make people who know you are their enemy, and what you are likely to do, follow you to the game park like some sheep?"

"Okay, first, you kidnap that American, the owner of the casino. He is old and slow. It should be easy. Greshenko will come after him and once they have been drawn off from the police, then you…"

"Then I what?"

"You do know it is not lawful to feed the animals?"

"I should break this law, you think?"

Irena smiled and poured another martini and held it out to Lenka. "It is such a small law to break. You will be forgiven."

"There is the other part."

"What other part?"

"This woman who is now in charge of the game rangers. My people say she is friends of the policeman who is nosing around. That will make it more difficult to enter the park even with our man in place."

"Leave her to me."

"You? What can you do?"

"She is a woman. I am a woman. We have things in common. Also, she has a daughter, did you know?"

"A daughter? So?"

"A daughter who is a student at their University in Gaborone and far away from her momma. She will be an easy mark for one of our people in the city to grab. We grab her. Then we tell Mamma to look the other way or the kid is very hurt. You, and the people you need—into the park you go, whenever you want. See, simple."

A tap at the door brought the conversation to a halt. Irena raised her eyebrows. Lenka shrugged and walked to the door. Alexei Grelnikov, a man of no discernible age or nationality, but who was clearly a person to be reckoned with, standing six feet seven and weighing three hundred and fifty pounds, give or take twenty, stood on the sill. He had few friends and was known to those who purchased his services only as Gur.

"Okay," he said and made no move to enter, "those guys at the airport? They went to the casino. They are like us but from America, yes, Rus? They are meeting. The blackie you sent over there to spy on them was sent away on an errand. He didn't know better and he went, so I don't have anything to tell you except they have guns. I couldn't find out where they got them. What you want me to do now?"

Irena studied the hulking figure at the door over the rim of her glass. "See if you can get one of them alone and pump him for answers. You don't have to be nice if you need to persuade him," she said and waved to Lenka to shut the door. Long conversations with Gur were rarely useful.

Lenka repeated what Irena said and closed the door. They heard Gur clump his way down the hall. There was no doubt in either of their minds that Gur's next stop would be at the casino where he would waylay one of Greshenko's people and beat some answers from him. They only had to wait. Irena poured another martini.

〉〉〉

Modise stood and gathered the beer bottles. "Time to go."

"So soon? Am I boring you, Modise?"

"Don't be so absurd. You never bore me, Sanderson. You are a person with infinite charms. I have to work. Something is telling me that there will be something happening and soon. I have stayed away from the casino because I cannot..." Modise caught himself. Sanderson was not privy to the plans worked out by Painter and Greshenko. The less she knew the better.

"Because...? Because you are cooking up something with that Russian and the American. That was why he came to the airport wearing that silly black suit. Were those friends of his who came in on that flight? I bet the bad man...Lenka, right? I bet he had people there too. Do you think they saw us leave together?"

Modise had not thought of that. If they saw them leave

together and made a simple addition in their heads, Sanderson could be in trouble. "Where are your son and your daughter?"

"Mpitle is in university and my son is working at the panel beaters in Kasane, why?"

"Nothing. I just needed to know."

"You just needed to know because, oh my gosh, you think they might try to get at you through me and my children."

"No, it is just a precaution and—"

"It is not just a precaution. I will call Mpitle and have her come home at once."

"That is not a very good idea. She is as vulnerable here as there and closer to them. I will make a call. She will be safe."

"How can you do that? You will put an officer with her twenty-four hours a day? Is that possible?"

Modise knew it probably wasn't, not within the authority he's been given. He could have someone watch at the times she'd be most vulnerable, but he could not justify three shifts of police protection on what the director would call a "Maybe." He'd need to think of something else. But what? He drew a blank.

"Kgabo...?"

"Let me think about this for a minute." It could cost him his job if he overreached. Resources were not what they used to be. Budgets were tight. No more hotel stays, personnel freezes, and there was the other thing: what would he do if he was not a policeman anymore? He was already out on a limb with this Greshenko plan. If it failed...He'd worked so hard to become the "Top Cop" he'd set as a goal so long ago. He looked at Sanderson. She wrung her hands. What to do?

He made the call. The voice on the other end asked him to repeat his request several times. "On my authorization," he finally snapped. How would the director react to that, he could only guess, but it was done. He had crossed a line. The question left to be answered: did it demonstrate good or bad judgment on his part? He'd find out soon enough. In the meantime Sanderson, her daughter, Mpitle, and her son, Michael, would have twenty-four/seven police surveillance. He told Sanderson what he'd done. She threw her arms around him and kissed him.

It would be another hour before, disheveled and grinning like a pair of teenagers, they drove out of the park. They would have been content, except that Modise's phone chirped. Without looking at the caller ID, he knew that something had gone wrong.

Chapter Sixteen

Seven men sat around the room, their shirts open and sweat dripping down their backs. They waited. A fan hummed and helped move the air around a bit. Adjusting the air conditioning was on Leo's punch list. He would deal with it later. At the moment his problem, well not his precisely, but the problem he chose to share with Yuri, had to take precedence. Finally he looked at his watch and shook his head.

"I don't know what happened to Modise, but I guess we start without him."

"Call him and ask him where he is and when he expects to be here," Yuri said. He cracked open more beers and passed them around.

"Who's Modise?" one of the newcomers asked.

"The local cop who's running the show."

"Where's Harry?" another asked.

Yuri did a quick head count. The man identified as Harry had slipped out to the washroom, but that had been twenty minutes ago. "I don't know. Maybe he fell in."

The men smiled at the old joke and turned their attention to Leo. He shrugged and pulled a whiteboard from the wall and uncapped a marker.

"Okay, here's how it is supposed to go. Yuri, here, is the top guy in this Bratva organization. You all are his gang. Is it gang, Yuri? What the hell do you call Bratva guys? Never mind. The real Russian baddie is this guy Lenka." He scribbled on the board. "He has it in his head that he wants to take over this hotel and apply muscle on the other Chobe River resorts. That would be these places especially." The marker squeaked as he listed in order the main hotels on the river. "If he does so, the government will have a huge problem. They have made it a priority to provide high-end tourism in the area and if these or any other thugs worm their way in, it will be a hard sell. People like Lenka are okay with rich tourists, but they also like volume. More money and a quicker return." Leo snapped the marker's cap back on. "The government, on the other hand, has a thing about crime in this country. They don't like it in any way shape or form."

"You're telling me they have no crime in this country? I don't believe it."

"I never said they didn't have it. What I meant was, they are really serious about keeping a lid on it and imported criminals is something they simply won't accept. Unfortunately, they tell us that Lenka has no outstanding warrants here or anywhere else, so they are stuck for the time being. Yuri, however, has a few old ones from his bad-boy days in Russia. The government, the cops intend to toss him out of the country unless he works with them to bring Lenka down. They didn't have much of a plan and it was pretty clear that if he did as they wished, he wouldn't make it past Wednesday. So, that's where you six come in. We persuaded the local cops to let Yuri run a sting. Instead of working for Lenka and ratting him out—that's the plan that guaranteed he wouldn't make it out alive—we convinced them to let him compete with Lenka. If the Russkie thought he had competition, say another Bratva group, we figured, he could be drawn into crossing a line or doing something rash sooner rather than later. It's not enough to simply run him out of the area. See, Lenka could duck across the border into Zimbabwe and, as far as the locals are concerned, disappear. They want him gone for good."

The door slammed open, bounced against the wall so violently that it nearly knocked the man standing in it off his feet. Harry had returned. His shirttail hung out of his pants. He had a red mark under his eye that was an hour away from becoming a magnificent shiner, and his knuckles were raw.

"Jesus, Harry, what the hell were you doing?"

"Greshenko," he said, "Do you know a big guy, maybe had a mother who was a silverback ape or maybe a buffalo? Oh, and maybe this guy really doesn't like you?"

"I hate to admit it, but I know a lot of people like that. Why?"

"Well, this one is duct-taped to one of your blackjack tables, Mr. Painter. Jesus, did he have a left hook."

"Are you going to tell us what happened, or what?"

Harry sat and took the damp cloth Leo handed him. He dabbed at his eye, and told them that he'd remembered he'd left his profile papers and passport in his room. He'd retrieved them and was crossing the parking lot when the door of a van slid open and this goon tried to haul him in. Instead, he's managed to drag the guy out and they'd had a scuffle.

"By the looks of that eye, I'd say it was more than a scuffle," Leo said.

"Yeah, well…anyway, so before I slapped the tape over his mouth, I asked who he was. He says he was going to kill me the next time we meet and I says that will be never because he's going to jail. He is, isn't he? I hate to think he'd be roaming the streets. So, anyway, like I said, we danced a two-step and I had to tune him up some. When your cop shows up, he might want to have some face time with that dude. Where is the cop, by the way?"

"Late. Yuri, you might want to have a word with the man taped to the table. Maybe he would be better used to send a message back to Lenka. Modise would love to have this guy, but if we hand him over, the connection between us and the cops will be blown."

"He and I will have a chat. You got it right, Leo. If we give him to the cops, even if we make it look like the cops arrested him, not us, Lenka will know and we're cooked. No, if we are going to be the people we pretend to be, this guy will have to go back to him in a Bratva way. We need to make sure Lenka knows that we mean business. He won't be happy. Maybe it will make him move sooner than later, huh? You call Modise and tell him what we got here and what we're doing. I'll be having my talk with the man. Did he say what his name was?"

"I asked and he just growled at me. Weird."

"Growled?"

"Yeah, grrrr…Like that."

"You know what you just did, Harry?"

"Growling?"

"No, to the man. If what you just said is what I think you said and I'm right about what that means, you just took out one of the most dangerous people in the whole Bratva nation. His name is Alexei Grelnikov but people know him as Gur, like grrrr. He is for hire and specializes in dismantling people on spec. Lenka has imported some very dangerous muscle."

"Good thing I didn't know. He might have taken me, given that reputation. You know what they say, 'ignorance is bliss,' though, I don't know, anybody who leads with a right in this day and age has to be less than current fighting-wise, you know."

Leo called Modise and asked where he was, and told him what had happened and what they planned to do. Then he listened and shook his head.

"Won't work, Modise. If you toss this guy in the clink, Lenka will figure it out. If we are going to act like bad guys, we have to play by their rules. Lenka would not call you if the situation were the reverse, if Yuri had sent the goon. He would have used him as a messenger or killed him on the spot. It's going to be close as it is. A real Bratva cell would mess him up a lot worse. Cut out his tongue, broken most of his bones. Something like that, and dumped him near to death on our doorstep. No, we'll do it our way."

He hung up. "Modise isn't happy. I think he thinks the operation has slipped out of his hands. Well, the truth is, with what's-his-name taped to a table out in the casino, I guess it has. Hell, it was just a matter of time before it did anyway. He's not dealing with poachers here or pickpockets and money launderers from Zimbabwe. These guys are really, really bad people. Okay, let's figure out what the message should be, bounce him around a little more and deliver him back to papa." Leo sat and wiped his brow. "I'm getting too old for this crap." He fumbled in his bush jacket for a cigar. "Who's got a light?"

Greshenko stood and walked to the door. "Leave this to me. None of you have the stomach for what has to be done. Okay, the message will be Gur. That's all. Gur in a bad way. Close the door behind me and bring that van around. We will deliver our message to Oleg Lenka tonight."

Chapter Seventeen

While Lenka and his woman stayed in the Mowana Lodge, his lesser operatives had to make do with a modified warehouse on the edge of Kasane. It had been Botlhokwa's headquarters previously and Lenka had simply usurped it along with the rest of the former boss' organization. It wasn't that bad compared to, say, a rondeval or one of the dilapidated shacks that housed the transients from Zimbabwe. It had running water and rooms that had been set up to offer some measure of privacy. A larger room with a desk and chairs filled the front third of the building. It did not have air conditioning, however, and the noonday sun beating down on the corrugated tin roof turned it into an oven. Large exhaust fans kept it from actually roasting its occupants and by evening it became livable, or nearly so. A large cooler with bottles of chilled beer helped. The men who found themselves domiciled there learned early on to find a shady spot outside during the day if they were not out and about doing the boss' business. Unfortunately for them, most of that business was pursued at night.

It was early evening, the sun just dipping below the horizon, when the van Gur had driven to the casino earlier, its horn bleating, arrived with a squeal of brakes and scattering gravel at the front entrance. Before anyone managed to squeeze through the door to see what or who had driven up, the van door had slammed opened and the badly beaten form of Gur had been dumped like a sack of potatoes onto the gravel. Whoever had driven it to the warehouse had disappeared.

Greshenko had sent his message. Lenka, when he heard about it minutes later recognized it for what it really was: not just a message, a declaration of war. He had not planned on that. He had not planned on a battered and, for the short run, useless Gur. What had started as a simple takeover of a local wheeler-dealer's business had escalated to something bigger and more dangerous. If he accepted the challenge, blood would be spilled. Not just the blood of the odd person here and there who had become an obstacle to his plans as before, but the blood of people close to him and, quite possibly, his own. The icy winters of St. Petersburg began to seem more appealing. To wage a war, unlike extortion, kidnapping, and episodes of assault and intimidation which characterized his operation before, altered its scale and scope dramatically. Inevitably confrontation with the police must be part of it.

In Russia, he'd managed to suborn the police. Enough rubles in the right pockets and the police were just another business expense. Here, in this strange country, he had yet to buy any policeman. That wasn't entirely true; there were one or two game rangers who would look the other way at night for a price, but they hardly counted as police. He wondered if Irena had been right about coming here. Was this place worth the effort? Johannesburg would be so much easier. He motioned to Irena to follow him and they left to see for themselves what had happened to Grelnikov.

He drove to the warehouse. He had a decision to make. People like Gur were hired help. They worked for money and would sell their services to the highest bidder. Greshenko had sent him back. Had he bought him first? Could he be trusted now? Lenka could not remember a time when someone had beaten Gur. What the hell kind of people had Greshenko brought to the Chobe?

The warehouse had not cooled down much when he arrived. The men waiting for him were sweating and uncomfortable.

They had cut away the tape that trussed up the bleeding Gur but he still lay on the floor gasping for breath. Lenka nodded to his next in command. Cszepanski poked at Gur with his toe. He moaned and took a ragged breath. Cszepanski reckoned he had a few broken ribs and one of them may have done some damage to one of his lungs. Gur gasped, coughed, and spat blood. Cszepanski tilted his chin at Lenka. Punctured lung. He didn't have to look for any other physical damage to know that this man would be useless for the next several weeks, probably longer, months even.

Lenka sat at the desk and pounded out an erratic beat on its surface with his hands. What to do? What to do with Gur? What to do about Greshenko? What to do next? Irena perched one hip on the desk and arched her eyebrows.

"So?" she said, "We lose a man. That is all. We change the timetable and move on."

"Timetable…yes. Move it, but what of Grelnikov?"

Irena shook her head, raised an eyebrow, and rolled her shoulder. "Kill him and feed the lions. You can't take the chance."

"Because?"

"Okay, because one, he is not able to do anything for you right now. He is broken and will be for a long time. Two, if Greshenko hasn't bought him and sent him back to us as an informer, he will be too timid now to do heavy work, the job you hired him to do, and three, even if he isn't either of those, he is the kind of man who will want revenge and go after Greshenko and then the police will be everywhere and we will be on plane to St. Petersburg. So, you get rid of him before he becomes a problem. Call our man in the park and dispose of him in the usual way."

Lenka stood and escorted Irena to the door. He turned to Cszepanski. "Do it." They disappeared into the night.

>>>

Cszepanski dismissed the remainder of the men in the room. When they were alone, he squatted down next to Gur. "You're a mess, old friend. I'm sorry I got you into this. The big man, make that the bitch, says I'm to kill you and drop you off in the bush to feed the hyenas. Okay, so you know I can't do much but, maybe I can buy you some time. Do you think you can walk a little?"

Gur muttered something Cszepanski could not understand. He helped him to a chair and poured a tumbler half full with vodka. "Here, drink this."

Beaten and wheezing, Gur wiped his mouth on his sleeve and downed the drink in one long swallow. He cast a bloodshot eye on Cszepanski. "Okay, you kill me or give me chance?"

"A little of both, maybe. I'll call Sami Nkola, tell him we have a pickup. He'll bring the boat over from Zambia and pick you up on the river. If you live long enough to meet him, he'll ferry you across. Then you're on your own, Okay?"

Gur shook his head. "*Ну, спасибо, что вы.*"

"Don't thank me, yet. You have to survive the trip, the river, and what comes next, Okay?" Cszepanski refilled the glass, gave it to Gur, and called a number in Zambia. He helped Gur to his feet, stuffed a fistful of hundred Pula notes in his pocket, and walked him to the van. Twenty minutes later they were at the river's edge west of the Chobe Game Lodge's Sundowner Bar. Gur struggled out. He stood gasping for breath. Cszepanski removed the clip from a nine millimeter automatic, ejected the shell in the chamber and dropped them at Gur's feet. He handed him an electric torch.

"You'll need this to signal Sami. Good luck." He drove off.

It took a great effort and not a little pain, but Gur managed to bend down and retrieve the pistol and clip. His half-shut eye made it too difficult to find the loose bullet. With a groan, he stood upright, slid the clip back into the pistol and racked a round into the chamber. He staggered toward the river. He found a tree to lean against and every five minutes or so he flashed the light toward the river. After a half hour, he saw an answering flash. Five minutes after that he huddled in the bottom of the smallest boat he'd ever seen and was on his way to Zambia. What he'd do there, he didn't know but one thing was certain; he would be back and Greshenko and that other man would be soon dead. Lenka and the woman, too. Cszepanski understood what he would need to do. That was why he'd emptied the gun before he gave it to him. Keeping silent that he was not dead meant staying alive yourself. Cszepanski would keep the secret. Cszepanski had a family somewhere. He would have to keep his mouth shut or Lenka would punish them and Cszepanski both. But the others? Gur would not take chances. He felt bad for Sami Nkola. He'd have to kill him as soon as he reached the opposite shore.

Chapter Eighteen

Her time had come and Kotsi Mosadi needed to find a safe place to birth her cubs. The previous year she'd enlarged a lair originally dug by a brown hyena she had chased off. The demands the pack had placed on her meant that she'd had no time to find a new place to lie up. Unfortunately for Danger Woman, the lair was two hundred meters away from an area that had only recently become a preferred place for a pride of lions to loll during the day. Also, the noisy and smelly things that roamed the park frequently crashed through the bush nearby. But now, as time was short, and despite its dangerous location, she had no choice but to return to it. She would exercise more caution when she entered and exited the area. She scanned the horizon and tested the air. She hesitated, shook her large head, snorted and, seeing and sensing nothing significant or threatening, entered her hideaway, her birthing chamber and, if she was not careful, quite possibly her tomb. She pawed out the old dirt, circled the narrow space, and settled down to whelp her cubs.

Downwind and a hundred and ten meters to the south in grass the same dun color as her coat, a lioness whose kill had been stolen by this same hyena a few nights earlier watched as it loped across the open space between her and the rise to the south. It disappeared for a moment into the bush and then reappeared. The lioness raised her head to track the hyena's progress. Her eyes glowed yellow in the afternoon sun and somewhere deep within her came a low rumble not unlike a cat's purr only deeper and more menacing. The scent had been distinctive. That hyena was about to give birth. She was not going anywhere soon. The lioness blinked and lowered her head back onto her paws. She would wait.

Ole Andersen had timed Kotsi Mosadi's gestation and knew she would be going to ground soon. Last year she'd made her lair in an embankment near the River Road. He expected her to do the same this year, but wanted to be sure. He drove his Land Rover to a spot close enough to watch, but far enough away so as not to frighten her off. The possible presence of lions did not worry him. The attack by a lion on a tourist in South Africa had come as no surprise to him. Caution around feral animals meant exercising a little common sense, a commodity missing in too many tourists. He'd fitted his vehicle with steel mesh in the windows and the camera mount on the roof hinged on the underside of the top. He manned it by standing on the seat and with the roof hatch back. In the unlikely event a lion would attempt to attack him, he had only to drop the camera down, slam the hatch shut and drive away. Ole was safe from any and all except an elephant. An elephant, particularly a bull with an attitude, could easily crush his vehicle and him in it. He made a point to avoid bull elephants, particularly those in musk. He thought others should, too, and said so frequently.

Now, he worried about Kotsi Mosadi. The hyena, his hyena, had put herself in harm's way. Last year, the lair placement had worked well, but lately the pride of lions that used to hunt farther westward had moved to this part of the bush, which could be a problem. Everyone knew that lions had no use for hyenas. If Kotsi Mosadi was careless even for an instant, one or another of them would dispatch her. He wished, not for the first time, that he could communicate with these animals he'd come to regard as his. If ever there was a time to be Doctor Dolittle and have a chat with her, it was now. But he wasn't. All he could do was watch, record, and hope the lions would stay preoccupied with other things. Perhaps a herd of kudu would wander by and the lions, their hunger sated, would ignore Danger Woman. He also knew that, hungry or overfed, if a lion had the opportunity, it would kill a hyena simply because it could.

He marked his spot on his GPS so that the camera angle would always be the same irrespective of the day the shot was made, and he settled back to wait. It would be days before he had his video completed.

Cszepanski sat his desk sorting papers. Two of Lenka's hires, a pair of Boer goons from Jo'burg, sat on the shabby leather sofa. They were the last of several he'd brought on board. Two others languished in jail at the moment. They were sent daily reminders of what would and very well could happen to them if they decided to cooperate with the police. Cszepanski had urged Lenka to put out a hit on them. Lenka said to wait. So they were waiting. He turned his attention on the two remaining Boers. One scowled at a graphic novel, his lips sounding out the words. The second had been cracking his knuckles for the last five minutes. Cszepanski thought if he didn't soon stop he would shoot him on the spot. Lenka would be angry, but it wasn't like these two were important or anything. Just hired muscle and idiots at that.

"So Shepan…Skiz…whatever you call yourself. How come you got out to the park, dumped the big ape, and back so quick last night? You must been speeding, yah?"

"Short cut, Hans. Listen, if you crack your damn bones one more time I will help you do it with the butt of this rifle."

"Okay, sorry. I know it's a bad habit. My Muttie was always on about how I would get arthritis if I do not stop. She's dead now so I can't tell her she was wrong. Oh, and my name is Johannes, and this fella is Jan."

Cszepanski rolled his eyes and turned his attention back to the pile of papers and miscellany on the desk. If he ended in Hell, which he reckoned a distinct possibility, he knew it would be filled with morons like these two, endlessly cracking their knuckles and mispronouncing his name. He wished them gone. He wished them dead. Neither of those possibilities was available. What had Lenka been thinking? Still they had their uses.

"Okay, Johann, or Joe or whatever, where is the nine mil that was here last night?"

"A gun is missing?"

"What did I just say? Which one of you apes took it?"

"You think one of us took a gun?"

"It was right here on the desk last night when I left. I come in this morning, you two are sitting here doing nothing, and it's gone. What am I supposed to think? Look, you morons are supplied with all the firepower you will ever need. There is no reason to pinch someone else's. What? Were you planning to sell it to one of the locals? If so, don't. They can't keep secrets and selling a gun like that is illegal and the police will be all over you like ugly on a gorilla. Got it?"

"By *Gott*, it wasn't me. Jan, did you take the pistol from the desk?"

"Who is missing a pistol?"

"Kepanz…he is. He says it is on the desk last night and now it's gone."

"Not me. I am not taking it."

"Well you birds better have a good story if Lenka comes and asks about it. He don't like people who rip him off."

The two Boers looked at Cszepanski dumbstruck and then at each other.

"Johann, you—"

"Me? It was you."

That took care of the missing pistol. There was an upside to keeping these oafs around after all. If Lenka ever wondered what had happened to the gun that he'd slipped to Grelnikov, he'd just shrug and kick one of these two to the curb.

Chapter Nineteen

When Grelnikov reached the riverbank in Zambia, he motioned Sami Nkola over and reached into his pocket. Sami, expecting a tip, smiled and held out his hand. Gur shot him twice and shoved him and his boat out into the current. The boat and disappeared into the river, Gur into the darkness. Late the following afternoon he staggered into Zimbabwe. He had one connection there. One would be enough. That, and the currency rate of exchange. Zimbabwe is the country which made it onto the Internet when it issued a trillion-dollar bill. It wasn't a stunt. Zim dollars are practically worthless—except in Zimbabwe.

Gur very soon discovered that the exchange rate had turned the wad of Pula notes Cszepanski had shoved into his pocket into several billion Zim dollars. He was rich. Rich enough to pay for medical care which would not find its way into any official record. Rich enough to tap into the black market and purchase a large supply of the painkillers he required. Rich enough to put up at a decent hotel where he could rest and mend, and rich enough to purchase his way back to Botswana when the time came. He intended to settle the score with Greshenko, who'd humiliated him, and Lenka, who'd betrayed him. His only miscalculation had to do with the healing process. Painkillers will mask symptoms, not remove them. His hotel stay would be shorter than he'd planned. Also, to his great disappointment, he was not able to persuade his friends from Moscow to join him. Had he been successful at that, what happened on the riverbank when he finally tracked down Greshenko might have ended differently.

Kgabo Modise did not like being late for his meeting, but here he was hurrying through the trees. He could blame Sanderson, but that would not be fair. Greshenko would just have to suck it up. That is how the Americans would say it. "Suck it up, pal." Before the operation slipped out of his control, Greshenko had been instructed to meet with him daily and report what he had learned from his activity acting as one of Lenka's henchmen. Everything was different now except the place to meet and that must change as well. The spot he'd selected, a clearing in the otherwise heavily forested riverbank seemed a safe place. Now, he wasn't so sure. The addition of six fake Bratva operatives and the complicated scheme that Leo Painter had cooked up made everything riskier, less certain.

The foliage near the river was dense and to the untrained eye, impenetrable. He found the clearing they'd agreed on as their meeting place but not Greshenko. Instead, Leo Painter sat on a fallen tree trunk with an unlit cigar between his teeth. "There you are, Inspector Modise. You know, I think I may be getting too old for this. You probably don't know it, but I had what the docs call a 'cardiac event' shortly after I came out here. I thought I'd up and died. My wife is all over me to come home to Chicago. She's not well. Age catches up with us all in the end. So, maybe she's right. If I'm going to die, back home in Chicago would make more sense. The thing is, I hate to quit, and even more than that, I hate to lose. I said I was going to build a damned casino out here and I'll be damned if some Russian goombah is going to stop me. Oh, by the way, sorry we had to call you off earlier. The goon Lenka sent to beat some information from one of our boys, sort of screwed things up."

Modise remained standing. He listened with half an ear to Leo. Americans, he'd decided, were much too outgoing and open for their own good. This man, for example, why did he think I should know about his heart attack or his wife's health or what she said, or even want to? He started to say something along those lines, but switched to, "Where is Greshenko?"

"Yuri is busy. More importantly, your bad guy, Lenka, has eyes on him twenty-four/seven. That makes it unwise for him to meet with you now. For the nonce, you will have to deal with me. We'll cook up something better but first, we talk."

"That was not the arrangement. Greshenko was to work with me, not you. I have stretched my authority to the limits with this arrangement you made to bring those men in from the States. Again, sir, I need to speak with Greshenko."

Leo shrugged and tossed the badly mangled cigar aside. A gray monkey that had been lurking nearby, dropped out of the trees, retrieved the cigar before it hit the ground, and bounded away.

"There goes a monkey with taste, Modise. That cigar was an H Upmann. It was a Cuban, Modise, surely you know cigars."

"I do not smoke, Mr. Painter, so, I do not know one cigar from another, nor do I care to. I came to this place to speak with Greshenko about what we are doing in the case of Lenka, not to you about cigars."

"Yeah? Sorry about that. Well, here's the deal, I will fill you in on all the important stuff. If you need to speak to Greshenko and don't trust me to adequately represent him, you will have to put someone else into play. Oh, and not one of those people you have pushing a broom around in the casino. All of those guys have been spotted, compromised, or turned. Pick someone you trust implicitly and would never be suspected to be connected to either Yuri or me. In the meantime, I will have to do."

Leo filled him in on what they'd finally decided to do with the hit man they called Gur. Modise took notes. He double underlined Gur, added a forward slash, and wrote: *Grelnikov— check with Interpol.* As he listened he realized how completely his operation had changed, he could only hope for the better. The plan laid out to him by Leo, and which he then relayed to the director, seemed complicated. Now, with all the elements in place, it seemed overwhelming. Before, it had been a nice, safe plan. This new iteration looked like the end game was to be the Russians' complete annihilation. Never mind deportation, burial services might be added to the to-do list. The director was not going to be pleased. Violence, even in the pursuit of justice, he held as a last and unwanted resort. These Americans and the "cowboy culture" they followed would opt for it as a first choice. Modise wrestled with whether he should tell the director, take the reprimand, and put this show back on the original script, or let it run and hope for an acceptable outcome, one that would discourage the next wave of Lenkas from trying to invade the Chobe. He sighed. There was something about being a "cowboy" that, much as he knew he should, he found difficult to resist.

"I will send someone to you with a message as to who will be my messenger. I am guessing it will be a woman. I am thinking that they will notice a woman not so much." Modise paused and frowned. "She will bring you some pens. You will need them."

"Pens? You mean like ballpoints? Why? Never mind, you have your reasons, I guess. Right. So, until we hear from you I will… Do you think that monkey will try to smoke my Upmann or eat it? Either way, I pity it. Probably kill him. Does that make me subject to arrest for abusing the wildlife? Or feeding them? If so, you know where to find me."

Leo stood, stretched, and wandered off through the trees. A few moments later, Modise heard an engine start and the sounds of a vehicle leaving the area. He waited another five minutes and then left himself. Well, Sanderson had always busied herself with playing at police work, he thought. Now he would give her a real assignment. Maybe it would cure her of this bad habit she had of putting her beak in where it did not belong.

He found Sanderson in her office. Derek Kgasa sat next to a window room reading the sports pages of a day-old copy of the local newspaper with the light through glass panes much in the need of a good wash.

"Hello, Derek, how is your uncle keeping? How is he getting along with the important official from Gabz visiting him this week?"

"Oh yes, it is Inspector Joseph Ikanya. He is very high up. The Director of the DIS must be very pleased with my uncle to have such an important person come and review his office."

"Oh yes, no doubt about that. It sounds very good for him. Excuse me, Derek, but do you suppose I might have a moment in private with the superintendent of the game rangers? There is the matter of some urgency I must deal with. It is not police business, you understand." Modise winked. After a brief moment of confusion, Derek's face brightened and he stood.

"I believe I will have an early dinner," he said and scuttled from the room.

"How did you do that, Kgabo? I have been trying to get rid of that goony bird every day since he arrived. He has no idea what his uncle wants him to do and is afraid to ask. So, how did you manage it?"

"It is a police secret. Speaking of police secrets, I have one for you."

Modise explained to her how the plan had changed and that she now had a task to do as part of the changes.

"I am to be the go-between? I will talk with this Greshenko person and then tell you what he says? Kgabo, that is crazy. They know that you and me...they know we are seen together."

"You are blushing, Kgopa."

"I am not, and do not call me that."

"No, you are right. You are many things, Sanderson, but your old uncles were wrong at naming you for the snail. You are *tau*, a lion, and I am sending you into the lair of hyenas. And yes, you are right. They know about you and me, but they also know that we know that they know."

"What?"

"Look, it is simple. Since I put a twenty-four/seven watch on you and your children, Michael and Mpitle, it is clear as crystal that we know they have figured out that you and I have become an item. That is what they call it in the gossip business."

"So?"

"So, they also know that we would never be so stupid as to use you as a messenger, knowing what we know they know, you see?"

"This is very confusing. They will believe that since we are aware that they know of our…relationship, they will not get in their heads that we are actually using me as a messenger, because that would be stupid and they don't think we are."

"Is that really clearer than what I said?"

"For me, it is. And from what I am hearing from those Russians, it is pretty clear they do think we are stupid."

"But not stupid that way, okay?"

"Okay, but why will I be seeing this Greshenko?"

"That is the good part. The American bought the new electric safari vehicles for his tourist guests. He has hired women to drive them. They must be trained. They must be familiarized with the rules of the park, the routes, radio frequencies, and so on. You or someone from your department will be going over there to do all this soon enough, I think. At least in a week. We have only moved up the timetable. You see?"

"And during this training I will have a chats with Greshenko in private but also out in the open, you could say, out of earshot."

"Not quite."

"What then?"

"You will sign in when you arrive. You will use a pen which you will absent-mindedly leave behind."

"The pen has a hiding place."

"Exactly, and if there is to be a return message, Greshenko will hand 'your' pen back but it will be an identical pen he has prepared."

"So I am to be James Bond. And when I am done with this pen?"

"Then we will have another picnic. We will have many picnics."

"Okay, Kgabo. But next time could we choose a place to picnic where the termites do not crawl into trousers while we are, um…engaged?"

"You are becoming warm under your collar, I think Sanderson."

Chapter Twenty

Irena had given in to the heat and stretched out in an all but invisible bikini on the settee on the balcony of her room with a pitcher of vodka martinis and a pack of the Turkish cigarettes to which she'd become addicted. Lenka said he had important business to attend to. That meant he'd be meeting with the men at the warehouse and blustering on about how he'd managed to become an important player in St. Petersburg. That would include boringly detailed accounts of the deals he'd made, the bodies left in his path, and the famous people whom he'd met. Irena knew that his stories were only partly true, but she never interrupted or discouraged these forays into his fantasy world with his cronies. Anything that kept him away and gave her a moment's rest worked for her. Lenka stormed into the room within a half hour.

"Sami Nkola has been shot, murdered."

"Who says?"

"Cszepanski says. He called to arrange a pickup. We have some people who want to visit Zambia but don't want the bother of visas. So, he calls and the boy at the other end says Sami is dead. He asks, 'How is he dead?' and the boy tells him, 'Shot with a pistol.' So, who is shooting our people over there? What does it mean? Have Greshenko's people infiltrated Zambia, too?"

"Calm down. Remember that Greshenko's men only just arrived. I think maybe, this Nkola, he is working for other people. He must have taken a job and it went bad, that's all. So, we find another boat. There are plenty of hungry Zambians and displaced Zimbabweans available for that sort of work. Promise them a motor for their boat, an electric one that doesn't make any noise and you will have plenty of people applying for the job."

"But, he was shot—"

"Forget Sami Nkola. These people, they are like flies. They die all the time. It is the jungle, yes? Things are shot. Animals, birds, people. It is their way."

She was correct about the pool of applicants, at least. Within hours after the word got out, several men with boats and monetary needs that trumped any moral commitments they must have entertained and applied for the job as a "Transfer Agent" for the famous Russian businessman. Lenka bought two just in case he lost another to the mysterious person who'd dispatched Sami Nkola. They were to stand by. They were free to engage in private business any way they chose but, whenever he called, they were to drop whatever they were doing immediately and make themselves available. For the two men selected, that posed no problem. Lenka, they understood, would need their services primarily at night. Most normal, that is to say legitimate river work, took place in daylight. If a boat operator knew what was good for him and his passengers, he stayed off the river after dark. To work the river at night was dangerous. In the day, you could see the hippos and pole away if they started for you. At night, it might be too late when you saw them, if you saw them at all. Everyone knew that they were the number one cause of homicide in Botswana. And then there were the crocodiles and tiger fish. If one didn't get you, another would. No, you stayed off the river at night.

Cszepanski said the primary boat man had an unpronounceable name, so he decided that he should be called "Bart." Even Oleg Lenka, who was not known for his sense of humor or perceptiveness, thought a statement from Cszepanski complaining about the difficulty in pronouncing someone's name an example of "the pot calling the kettle black." Cszepanski did not laugh. Irony does not play well in the world of mobsters. Bart was put to work immediately. Lenka had people and merchandise to move.

Mpitle stared at the empty bed across from her own. What had happened to her roommate? Shana's grades were never very good but not so bad she would be asked to leave the University. Had she quit and gone home? She did say she felt homesick once or twice. Shana's closet had nothing left in it but some empty hangers and a lone sock which Mpitle recognized as one of her own. A knock at the door to the corridor and immediately it swung open. A woman lugging two large plastic bags and a suitcase entered, dumped her belongings on the empty cot, waved and left. Mpitle started to say something to the empty room. Minutes later the stranger returned with more bags and a young man who had one arm covered with tattoos. He carried a large box filled with books.

"This is Kimbo," the strange woman said. "Put the stuff over there, Kimbo, and scoot."

"I am not invited to the party? We could get something to eat and then…"

"No party, goodbye."

Kimbo left. The woman sat on the only clear spot on the bed and smiled. "I am sorry. You seem confused. You are Mpitle Sanderson, yes?"

"Yes. Who are—"

"I am Kopano Lekgwamolelo, your new roommate."

"My new roommate? What happened to Shana?"

"She said to say she was sorry. Nothing personal but, she had a chance to move in with her cousin. She thought you'd understand."

"That's it? She's sorry?"

"That's what she said."

"Okay, I guess. So, you are to take her place. You are a student here?"

"A few graduate courses. Just temporary. One term, maybe two. So, Mpitle, what are you studying?"

"Engineering, but I don't know. The math is—"

"My grandpa says to me, Kopano, math is a man's work. He is from the previous century. For that, I took calculus and received the highest grade in my form. Do not let it defeat you."

"Yes, thank you. Umm…Oh, golly. Kopano, there is something you should know before you unpack."

"Yes?"

"I received a call from my mother. She says I am to be watched by a police constable twenty-four/seven. I expect there will be some person in a uniform hanging around all the time. If that is a problem for you—"

"Why would that be a problem for me?"

"I was thinking of your boyfriend. He is—"

"Not my boyfriend. *No mathata.* So, we will be great friends."

"Yes, I hope. Oh, golly, I forgot. I was not supposed to say anything about the constable to anybody. You will not mention it, okay? Besides, once a constable starts following me around, everyone will know anyway."

"It will be our secret."

Lenka was back to pacing. "We need to know what the police are doing over at that casino."

Irena rolled her eyes. "They are there?" Irena searched among the bottles on the side board. "We are out of vodka. Send down for some."

Lenka called the desk and ordered two bottles to sent to the room, "No, but they were."

"I told you we should have brought the phone man with us when we came up from Cape Town, but you said we don't need him. If we tried to have their phones tapped they'd find out, you said."

The boy with the vodka arrived. Lenka handed him a tip and closed the door.

"Wait." Lenka held up a hand and listened. He gripped the knob and jerked the door open and peered out. "No one. I thought I heard...never mind. I said there are almost no land lines in this country and as nearly as I can make out, the police here depend on cell phones."

Lenka drifted to the door and jerked it open again. He searched the corridor looking for eavesdroppers. He slammed the door shut. "Okay, so tapping mobile phones is not the same as land lines, Renee. Even if we brought him here to set up a...what is the thing called? Ah, set up an IMSI-catcher in this country, it would take time. And if the police phones are encrypted, we learn nothing. For now, we have people eavesdropping. It's the best we can do. Whose phones do you want cloned? Modise the policeman's?"

"Why not? He is the person who most wants you back in Russia. It would be nice to know what he is doing. Also Greshenko. Clone his, too."

"Sure why not? You are joking. Tell me, how do we get so close to either man that he will give us his phone?"

"That woman, the ranger person. She will do this for us."

"She will? How? She is not for sale."

"She will not know she is doing it. You plant the software on her phone while she is busy with something else and then, when she is with the policeman, we turn it on remotely and it is done."

"Okay, how do we plant this software on her phone?"

"You can leave that to me. Bring in the phone man."

Chapter Twenty-one

Sanderson inspected the box of ballpoint pens Kgabo Modise had had left for her. His instructions were to divide them into two groups and deliver the one half to Greshenko. She was warned that under no circumstances was anyone to see the exchange. There were no instructions on how that was to be done. She didn't like the pens either.

Apparently, the pens had a message or logo on them at one time. Whatever message had been printed on the barrel, it had been poorly removed with sandpaper or a nail file. Were these police department pens? Modise had said they were economizing, but were they really that stupid? These pens will fool no one, she thought. She shook her head and muttered about the tendency men had to take shortcuts and cause trouble for those who had to clean up after them. She fished around in her desk drawer, the one where she kept the items Charles Tlalelo called her "lady things." She found a bottle of nail polish remover. Why she had that particular item in the drawer, she could not say. She did not use nail polish. She applied a thin coat to the scratched portion. When it dried the barrel was smoother, the scratches and scrapes certainly less noticeable.

It wasn't easy ignoring the reek of acetone but, she managed to coat all of the pens. She let them dry and then put half of them in an envelope which contained copies of the park rules regarding vehicular traffic. Modise had enclosed his first message in one of the pens. She put all but that one of the remaining half in the desk with the nail polish remover. The one with the message she tucked in her pocket and set out for her appointment with the new safari guides and, incidentally, Greshenko.

So, now she had an official position as a police operative. She didn't know whether to be excited or afraid. It is one thing to talk about how things should be done, another to do them. Modise said these Russian gangsters could be very violent and brutal. What if they figure out what she is up to? Modise said he was deputizing her. She was not sure what that meant either. It sounded official. Should he have given her a badge? Perhaps a set of shoulder flashes would be better. Either way, she thought she needed some sign that made her new position official. She would ask him the next time they had their picnic. She ought to have a ribbon at least.

As arranged, Greshenko waited for her at the casino office. She handed him the fat envelope and made sure he knew he was to distribute the contents to his drivers. He nodded and gestured toward four women in khaki uniforms standing off to one side. He handed her a clipboard and she made a show of scanning the form attached to it. She signed at the bottom, and returned the clipboard to him with her pen slipped under the clamp. He took it, placed it on the desk, and turned to the women whom he introduced. Sanderson took them into a side room set up as a classroom and began her instruction. If anyone had been watching, however closely, they would have neither seen nor heard anything that could possibly link Sanderson and Greshenko.

After the session ended, Greshenko stopped her as she was about to exit through the door.

"Here, Mma Michael, you forgot your pen."

She smiled at that. She thanked him, pocketed the pen and left. An hour later, she had lunch in the park with Kgabo.

It had begun.

Tumelo Carter was one of the four drivers hired by the casino and enrolled in Sanderson's training class. Tumelo had a brother,

Jik, who was, in a word, broken. Drug addiction is not the great problem in Botswana as in its neighbor, South Africa, but it exists and those caught up in it have fewer sources to sustain their habit. Tumelo's brother had been found out by Lenka's people. He thought he had won a lottery when they approached him and offered him a job. The supply of drugs now seemed endless and the cost fair. Fair meant he became a dealer. His newfound friends asked only one favor in return. It was a small favor. He was to persuade his sister to do a job for them. If he agreed, his position in the organization would be secure. If not…what would become of him or his sister should he refuse was never stated. It didn't need to be. He hesitated. There were problems, he'd said. He hadn't any contact with his sister for nearly a year. His contact shrugged and left. When his supply of drugs ran out, he had to face the reality that soon he would have no money and no chemical support. He agreed to talk to his sister. Yes, he would see to it she did as he asked. And really, what possible harm could come from simply borrowing someone's phone for a minute and exchanging the SIM card? Nothing, that's what. He doubted it would even be considered illegal.

When Jik finally tracked down his sister, she was less than happy to see him. Tumelo recognized the signs. Her brother had found a new source to feed his addiction. Any hope he might come to his senses and find his way back home were lost. So sad. He dismissed her lecture and told her he needed her to do something for him. It was really important; he'd said Tumelo asked who he was working for. He said it didn't matter.

"If I do not know who I am doing this favor for or I am not doing it."

"It is for me, Tumelo."

"No, Jik, it is not for you. It is for the people who supply you with the *moshutele* you are shoving up your nose, or is it in the veins this time?"

He pleaded, he begged, he threatened. She only came around when he told her he would die if she didn't do this thing. Yes, she would try. She emphasized the word, try. She would try to get her hands on Ranger Superintendent Sanderson's phone and switch the card.

"Then, I never want to see you again. You have disgraced your family, the village, and the tribe. You are *tshedisa molewane*, Jik. Nobody will speak to you. Look at what you have become. You live in that place with those terrible people. If you promise to go to a rehab program, I will do this. Will you?"

He promised he would and then he'd be out of her life forever if she did this one last thing. She knew that would never happen. He would be back to beg, to steal, or do whatever his habit demanded of him. That night she wept for her lost brother.

The following day, at her training session, she asked to borrow Sanderson's phone. Her phone, she said had a flat battery. Sanderson gave it to her without questioning why. Tumelo stepped from the room, cracked open the phone and removed one card, inserted another. After the card was exchanged and the phone returned, Sanderson made a call. She frowned when she did so and Tumelo feared she'd been found out. Nothing happened. After the training session, Tumelo called and reported the switch had been made to her brother who in turn passed the information on to his contact.

When the news made it up the chain to Irena that the game ranger's phone was set to clone the policemen's, she said that they were to reward the boy. They were to give him something special in his ration of drugs. One good deed deserved another, she said.

The next morning the Kasane police found Jik Carter dead of an apparent overdose. His body lay sprawled in the tin-roofed shack he shared with his girlfriend. The needle was still in his arm. The girlfriend was not dead, only nearly so. Jik, for all his faults, was a sharing person. His girlfriend would be a sharing person, too, but in a different way when she came out of her coma. It wouldn't help much in the investigation at the time, but when the file on Lenka was finally closed, it would be a useful addition.

Chapter Twenty-two

Superintendent Mwambe had a bad day, at least for him it had been. The presence of the officials from Gaborone had set him off. He knew what people in the capitol thought of him, that he was old, overweight, and inefficient. Some nights, when sleep eluded him and his bones ached, he conceded that the impression might have some merit. Admitting the possible truth to it did not, however, mean that he could not function in his job. No, he would admit it; he was not a modern man. He remained "old school' and it worked for him. Inspector Joseph Ikanya, at least, understood that. The two of them had conversations about how times had changed and this intruder from Gabz who'd arrived with Inspector Modise had agreed. He did not share the same level of negative as Mwambe. He sighed. This one thing he knew; no one worked a crime scene better than he did. He never boasted about his work. He knew that when he'd had serious crimes, he'd managed them. So, why did the director believe he needed help from Modise? Clearly down in Gaborone they did not understand. This far north, things were to be approached differently, had to be dealt with in a manner more nearly suited to the locale and its people. Why couldn't they see that?

He thought of his nephew, Derek. Derek was his only living relative. Mwambe was a very private person when it came to his personal life. His wife of thirty-five years had died four years previously. There had been no children. He regretted that as much as anything he'd failed at in life. It had been his failure. The doctor said it had something to do with acquiring a serious case of mumps as an adult. Really? How that could be was beyond his comprehension. Mumps were in the jaw, not…there. His wife never said a thing but, her disappointment filled every room every day and every night. For twenty-five empty years his failure to father children was the "gorilla sitting on the sofa." To be childless in his time brought with it head-shaking from neighbors and talk behind their backs. Whether the cause of their unhappy state fell to him or an act of God, it was their unhappy lot nevertheless. After a while, she took to drink, he to overeating. Her response to their problem killed her. His made him a local joke, the fat policeman. Well, there could be no fixing that now. He had to travel on, do his job and wait. Wait for something. He couldn't rightly say what that something would be.

His musing was shattered by his phone ringing. He started to admonish Derek for not picking up and then he realized he'd sent his nephew over to spy on Sanderson. He lifted the receiver.

"Yes?"

Inspector Ikanya from Gaborone wanted to meet. What now?

Their picnic took place in the trees by the river once again. It was safe enough. Even though they were in the dry season, this spot, because of it steep bank, would not be visited by thirsty animals coming to the river to drink, nor would those in the river likely be climbing out to threaten them. Sanderson handed Modise the pen she'd received from Greshenko and watched as he unscrewed the barrel and retrieved its small scrap of paper with Greshenko's message.

"What does the Russian say?" she asked.

"He tells us…Wait. You are not cleared to know this."

"I am not cleared? You declared me the deputy. I am the carrier of these messages both to and from. I am the taker of the risks. What do you mean I am not cleared, Modise?"

"I mean, the director would not wish you to take even greater risks by knowing the contents. What you don't know—"

"Can't hurt me? That is great nonsense, Mister Policeman.

If I know what the message is, I can anticipate what is coming next and maybe help you to avoid danger."

"I am sorry, Kgopa…Sanderson. It is for the best. Besides I am in very deep on this operation and if it fails, if it becomes costly, it is likely I will lose my position. I have stepped over the line and the director is not happy with me."

"Well, you can tell the director he is being stupid and you can tell him I said so."

"That is never going to happen."

"No? I don't like it and that is that. Another thing, why don't I have a badge? I am the Deputy, I need a badge."

"There are no badges."

"Then a ribbon or a card with my picture that says I am a Deputy Constable."

"Sanderson…"

"It's not fair, Modise."

They sat in silence, Sanderson pouting, Modise wondering if he shouldn't say something about the contents of the Greshenko message. Sanderson possessed a cheerful nature which could never be suppressed for long. She turned to Modise. "Okay, there are no badges and I am not to be trusted with secrets, just used as the messenger baboon. We are not done with this conversation, Inspector Modise. So okay, here is one for you. Didn't you ask me to tell you if anything odd happened at the casino?"

"I did. Has something odd happened?"

"What would you describe as odd?"

"Odd? I don't know, exactly. Something unexpected. Something ordinary in an extraordinary place. Something somebody said that doesn't quite match up with what is going on, that sort of thing"

"I see. Well, here is something very ordinary happening in a very ordinary way that I am still wondering about. One of the trainees asked to borrow my phone. She said her battery had gone flat."

"And?"

"And, I let her have it and she was out of sight and then she returned it."

"And that is odd, how?"

"I saw her talking on her phone outside after the session. I don't think she had her phone on a charger while we were in class. I do not think she has a self-charging battery. Why does she need to borrow my phone?"

"Did she see you seeing her on her phone?"

"No."

"Good. May I borrow your phone for a moment?"

"Your battery is also flat?"

"No. I just need to see your phone."

She handed it to him and sat back to watch. He snapped off its back and removed the SIM card. He squinted at it for almost a minute and then replaced it.

"This is a new one," he said. "They are after cloning phones."

"What? How can you tell?"

"I have seen this before. We will use them sometimes in the pursuit of criminals. See, this card is identical to the one you purchased but has an addition. Your phone is always on even when you think it is off. It will not draw down your battery very much, but you will notice you must recharge more often."

"It is on now?"

"Yes."

"So people can hear what I am talking about all the time?"

"No, it's not that kind of on. There is a card programmed to do that but, this is not one of them. No, this one is different. It is set to search for another phone. Mine for example, and it will then steal the information from my phone and store it. Then, you will receive a wrong number call and while you are saying 'so sorry' to the caller, all my settings and so on will be downloaded to that phone. Then, the next time I receive a call, that other phone will ring as well and the holder of that phone, the clone, will be able to hear everything I say."

"This is true?"

"Absolutely."

"I am so sorry, Kgabo. I didn't know. Why would that nice girl do this thing?"

"There is nothing to be sorry for. You couldn't have known, in the first place, and you have done us a favor in the second. The girl is either one of them or she is in their power somehow."

"You will arrest her for this foolishness?"

"No, I think we will leave her in place. She could be very useful to us now that we know what she is up to. Also, if we did pick her up, Lenka would know and assume, correctly, that we know what they did to the phone. I want him and his people to believe they were successful making the switch."

"I have done you a favor? How is that?"

"Well, I will see to it that you clone the 'correct' phone. We will set up a dummy phone and fill their ears with buffalo droppings. Sorry, with false information. That way we can send them on many wild goose chases."

"Goose chases?"

"False trails."

"Oh. What if this thing, this cloning has already happened? Maybe it is too late."

"The phone they wish to clone must be on and you must be within a very few feet of it for that to happen. I did not want our meeting be disturbed. My phone has been off since you arrived and is sitting in my coat pocket in the truck. So, the cloning hasn't happened and even if it had, it would be of no use to them. I have two phones, Sanderson, one for personal use, one for official business. The official one is encrypted and is off. Even if they had cloned that one, they will know nothing. The personal one? Well let's just say, be careful what you wish to tell me about your love life."

Sanderson punched him on the arm. "You know that I am not one of those women who does things like that."

"No sexting?"

She smacked him again.

"So, for the time being, let us be careful what we say on our phones. When we return to Kasane, I will set up the false phone. Perhaps your friend Mwambe will operate it for us."

"Superintendent Mwambe? Kgabo, he is like one of the elephants grazing in the bush, always in search of food. Why would you give such an important job to him?"

"Ah, you are almost right. Not the elephant, he is like a hippo and what do we know of hippos? If they are set up right, they are very, very dangerous. Do not underestimate the large policeman. He may be reluctant to move into this century, and wishes crime would occur somewhere else than in his jurisdiction, but he is not incompetent when challenged. He will do the job." Sanderson shook her head. Modise must know something she didn't, for sure. "Time to go back to work," he said. It didn't sound like he believed it.

"So soon? Are we truly finished with our picnicking now, Kgabo?"

He turned, saw the twinkle in her eye. "Maybe not just yet."

Chapter Twenty-three

For his part, Joseph Ikanya made a very passable director on the "cloned" phone Modise set up. Superintendent Mwambe sounded very convincing as the local police. He should have. He *was* the local police. The two men, happy to be involved in a real way and in what they described as "hi-tech" police work but also, well out of harm's way, began a series of sporadic calls back and forth intended to distract and misinform Lenka's people. They would do so at odd hours and irregular intervals for the next several days. If Lenka was listening, he would have discovered several interesting things. He would hear that numerous people with questionable visas were attempting to enter the country and join the personnel at the casino. That there was an emergency at the border with Zambia which involved a shipment of liquor that had not been properly taxed. They might have wondered at the report that game rangers were being armed with side arms and posted to secure the park from unauthorized entry, specifically to curtail the dropping of corpses in the bush. Lenka's people in the Ranger Service said they knew nothing about that. They would ask. One did and disappeared. There were references to operations with names like "Lion Strike" and "Baboon Watch." Mwambe made that one up.

They also would have heard that the American who owned the casino had left the country and that the ownership of had been transferred to a Botswana-based corporation. That message happened to be the only truthful one. Leo Painter had flown back to Chicago to attend to his sick wife. As his health was also questionable and his return to Botswana uncertain, he'd incorporated the operation and placed Greshenko as its COO. Greshenko had objected. He felt that he'd done nothing to deserve the position. Leo said he agreed. He would do it anyway, he said, because… well, because he wanted to and because he could.

The news came as a surprise, but a good one. Modise wanted Lenka to know that the American was out of play and that his only point of entry to the casino now would have to be through Greshenko. This move by Painter, he realized, had both good points and bad; good because assuming control of a corporation should be easier for Lenka than wresting it from a private owner. The bad part: it significantly reduced Modise's hold on Greshenko. He wondered if that hadn't been Painter's intent all along. Well, what was done was done. He would worry about Lenka's next moves later. At least, Modise figured, he'd baited the hook. Now, he would do some fishing.

The intercepted phone calls confused and worried Lenka's sources in Cape Town and Gaborone. They could not confirm any of the information in them except the one concerning the American's departure. Lenka struggled with who or what to believe. In the past, the sources in Gaborone and Cape Town had been spot on. Now he weren't so sure. Had any of the information they had forwarded up to Kasane previously been correct? What was going on? One of the men monitoring the wire traffic in Gaborone suggested that because the data at his end and that coming from the cloned phone seemed so wildly different, it might be a diversion. He suggested that the police may have tumbled to the scheme to clone the phone and were deliberately feeding them disinformation. Lenka dismissed the idea out of hand. He declared these local people hadn't the brains or capability to pull off something as sophisticated as that. Bigotry frequently creates its own punishment.

The upshot of all this was that Lenka decided to retrench. He would wait for Greshenko to make the first move. He would go on the defensive. It was not a position he played well. Irena took him aside.

"What are you thinking, Oleg?" she asked. Aggressive behavior, bullying had brought him this far, why would he change now? "You must move quickly now. You see? You can grab the casino so easily. Do it now while the American is away and this company he set up is still new."

He shook his head. "You don't understand, Renee. We will soon be outnumbered. We will wait and see how many people Greshenko brings in. In the meantime, I will bring the men up from Cape Town and Gaborone. We need reinforcements."

"What? Reinforcements? How can you believe that and at the same time tell everybody that the natives aren't worth worrying about?"

"Something is not right here and I want to fix it, that's all."

"If you do that, what will hold the groups left in those places together? If they are gone from there, we lose the little bit we have built. We were going to make a base, remember? We need to cover the country from Gaborone. Oleg, you are going to be too thin in Gaborone to hold onto anything. The men at *Ресторан* are not enough to keep something in place. What will we have there? The old man, a cook, and manager, that's what we are leaving behind. Not even the waiters. What can they do if we need something done in Gaborone? We pull the street people and then what? No, you must go after the casino now. No calling in reinforcements. No waiting."

"It is only temporary. You will see. When he sees what we have against him, he will be the one to back down. He will come begging."

Irena threw up her hands. "You are an idiot."

Lenka backhanded her and she tumbled on the sofa. He would be sorry later. He always was. She stood and left. Later, she pulled out her phone, went to online banking and wire transferred all of the money she'd skimmed from his business and had dumped into a local Barclay's Bank to her account in Geneva. She had finagled the combination to the safe from him the last time he'd lost control but reckoned it would not be the right time to clean it out. She hoped he'd realize what he'd done and ask for forgiveness. If Lenka's contrition was great enough, she might squeeze some diamonds from him. Diamonds, everybody knew, were a woman's best friend. A blond American actress sang that song at a cinema she'd attended a long time ago. The woman had a big mouth and sang it in English but the words were sub-titled in Russian on the screen, *Алмазы, а девочек лучший друг.* She would make some…what do the bratty children on America TV say? Some BFFs. Yes some new best friends, the sparkly kind.

Leo's sudden departure and amazing gift left Yuri Greshenko in a state of euphoria which quickly evaporated when he realized that he now had an even larger target on his back. Before, his fate had oscillated between dead and deported. Now the dead part seemed more likely than the deported bit. But, more than that, he missed the gruff old American with his plans and schemes, his endless stories about the rich and powerful, and the uses he'd made of both. He hoped he'd come back soon, but in his heart he knew he'd seen the last of Leo Painter.

He turned his attention to his current dilemma: what to do about Oleg Lenka and Modise the policeman. He pulled a scrap of paper from the desk drawer and scrawled a note which he placed in the barrel of one of the pens supplied by the police. The game ranger woman would be arriving soon and he wanted something in writing from the authorities guaranteeing him permanent residency if he fulfilled his end of the bargain. He hadn't asked for it previously. At that time, he was in no position to bargain. He felt he was in a stronger position to do so now.

"No guarantee," he muttered, "no goodbye to Lenka." He still had options. He was the chief executive officer of a Botswana corporation. He had a legitimate claim to remain in spite of his previous status, or non-status. And those men Leo imported to play at being Bratva agents, well they would be happy to leave all this behind as well. Take them out of play this late in the operation and the police had nothing. Less than nothing.

Even from far away America, Leo had demonstrated the genius that had made him the CEO of the second largest power and mining conglomerate in the world. The one he had left to others to run in order to build a modest casino/hotel in Botswana. A facility which now sat completed and ready for business on the banks of the Chobe River under the capable stewardship of his odd friend, Yuri Gresenko.

So, good news, bad news. Yuri relaxed and celebrated the former with a cold beer. The bad he'd ignore.

〉〉〉

Michael snapped his out-of-date mobile phone shut. He did not seem happy. Sekgele waited for what came next.

"Sekgele, that was my mother calling. She says she is not supposed to be telling me this thing and then she tells it to me anyway."

"What is she saying, exactly? Michael, you are worried. Tell me what she said."

"We are being watched round the clock by the police."

"Watched? Why? We are doing nothing wrong. We are planning on a wedding. What is so wrong with that? My father is having us watched by police? Is that it? How can he do that?"

"It's not that, Sekgele. There is some trouble brewing here. It's not your father who brought the police. My mother set it up. There is the business with the Russians trying to move in on Rra Botlhokwa's old business and she worries about that. At least that is what she says. It is not too clear to me. Why does what is happening to that old crook's corrupt operation have anything to do with us?"

"Who is Rra Botlhokwa?"

"You don't know? No, you wouldn't. Your father sent you to school with the nuns. Back in the day, among his other enterprises, Botlhokwa was a thief and a smuggler. He seems pretty small-time now but then, he was someone to deal with in the Chobe. His real name was Livingston Boikobo. He changed it to Botlhokwa when he became a famous gangster, you could say, so he is Rra Botlhokwa, in English, Mister Big, see?"

"Did you ever have something to do with this Rra Botlhokwa? You weren't a smuggler or something? Are you not telling me something?"

"No, of course not. I was too sick to do anything even if I had wanted to. And I surely did not want to. I had some school mates who…never mind. Not me. Now, with you here, when do I have time for crime?"

"But, your mother says we are being watched by police because of that? Do you believe that? Or is it because of…you know?"

"I don't know. No, I take that back. My mother is many things but devious is not one of them. So, if you see a police constable peeking in the window, do not worry. He is here to protect us."

"You are being a joker, Michael."

"I certainly hope so."

Chapter Twenty-four

Birthing four cubs had not been easy for Danger Woman. Perhaps it was her age. She had reached that time in life which, in hyena years, would be reckoned as middle age. She held the position as the pack leader as much for her cunning as her fierce nature, a cunning acquired from years of watching and waiting and holding off challengers to her position. That activity had also taken its toll in a leg that never quite healed from the gash put there by a younger female eager to take Kotsi Mosadi's place. Another year or two and the youngster would have won. In the animal kingdom, youth has no more patience with the limitations of age than do the humans who hunt them. She strained to keep pace with those younger pack members, many of which were her own offspring, a fact that in no way made them less competitive or more loyal. One slip, one more debilitating injury, no matter how slight and she would be displaced, possibly killed. Family is not a concept that carries the same meaning in the wild as it does in the living rooms of people.

By the time her offspring had made their way into the world, Kotsi Mosadi was exhausted. The litter of four, two males and two females quickly became a litter of three when one of the males died in the night. The next day she pushed its stiff little body into the deep end of her burrow and scratched some earth over it. This would be the last year she'd use this place to birth her cubs. She nuzzled the three remaining. She had not eaten in three days and realized she must do so if she were to provide nourishment for them. She would have to leave her lair and hunt. Hunt alone.

Her pack would be scattered across the park, the females laid up in burrows like hers replenishing the pack's numbers, the males wandering about, some hunting in scraggly groups, some by themselves. Until she returned and called them into line, the pack posed no real danger to any of the larger herbivores in the park. That would change when she and the other females returned with their offspring. But that might even stretch out for a few weeks. Definitely not soon.

It is an entirely different operation to hunt alone than as a team. A pack provides options. A pack can herd an animal into a corner. A pack can attack a prey larger than any individual within it. Hunting alone meant preying on smaller game, scavenging, or running down the old and the weak. Danger Woman had done it many times before. She could again. She put her head out of the lair and tasted the wind. A breeze, slight, almost nonexistent stirred her whiskers. The little that wafted through the bush convinced her that the lion pride had abandoned the area. No sleek lioness or her cubs lolling in the grass to the south today. She chortled at her own cubs. They would not move until she returned.

She heaved herself out of the burrow and trotted toward the river. Hunting alone meant finding easy prey. Thirsty animals would go to water to drink. The act of drinking was the one vulnerable moment in an animal's daily routine. Head down, back to the bush, eyes focused on the water, they would be taken from the river by a drifting crocodile which would explode onto the bank and pull in anything, or attacked from the bush by a fast moving hyena. Danger Woman would feed at the river.

She loped across the dusty veldt heading north toward the forested riverbank.

Ole Andersen, his camera rolling and with its zoom capability engaged, followed Danger Woman across the open savannah immediately in front of him. She paused, tested the air, and trotted out of sight. He guessed she would head to the river. If he guessed correctly, he could set up downwind from the spot and be in a position to film her next move. He hinged the camera back into the Land Rover and drove across the bush making sure he did not disturb Danger Woman. These images of the leader of the most successful pack of spotted hyenas would make a classic documentary. He might be able to sell it to *National Geographic.* Of course they had been bought up by Murdoch now, so who knew? If not, perhaps some American public broadcast television outlet could buy it. Who was he kidding? It might never see the light of day. Still, capturing this hyena and her pack was his passion. Who cared if fame did not follow? At least he would include it with the rest of his application when he applied for renewal of his research grant. Few researchers had accumulated so much data on hyenas, much less the life cycle of a single one. Ole had been taping Kotsi Mosadi since she was a cub. It would be his crowning achievement.

He knew better than to take anything for granted. Unlike *homo sapiens,* the wild was wholly unpredictable. What seemed fixed and certain one day could be wildly chaotic the next. Lions were said to avoid elephants. They might attempt to take down a calf that had wandered too far from the herd but, the conventional wisdom declared that, if attacked, an elephant would sound a distress call and bring in the entire herd. Combined, the elephants would crush the attacker unless they were quick and raced away from the area. For years researchers accepted that as truth. Then one filming crew that had been following an elephant migration in Kenya captured at night a sequence in which a pride of near to starving lions took down an elephant and killed it within the hearing and comprehension of the rest of the herd. So, there were no rules, only tendencies, probabilities, and legends.

Ole counted on the ferocity and cunning of Kotsi Mosadi to survive for a few more years. When she faded, he would film her displacement from the leadership of the pack and her eventual demise, most probably initiated by her own kind. He hoped that would not be soon. He had grown fond of this ugly animal.

The director might be economizing, but Modise didn't think that meant he must do so as well. Not on his own time and with his own money. He sat at the restaurant waiting for Sanderson. He'd asked for and been granted a secluded corner. Lenka's people could be around and he couldn't be too careful. Still, meeting at the river had its moments, for sure, but, Sanderson deserved better than sandwiches and warm beer out of the back of her Land Rover. They'd had a proper date once, at this very hotel and it had ended very well. He smiled at the memory. Of course it had been at night and Sanderson wore a dress and a scarf. He especially remembered the scarf. This time, sad to say, they would have to make do with a luncheon. Not the same thing, but there would be other opportunities for something more appropriate after this Russian business ended. He surveyed the room. No sign of her yet.

Their relationship had progressed past what his grandfather would call "a nudge and a tickle" to something with more substance. The question he had to struggle with: how can this ever work? Sanderson is the first woman to attain the position she holds. She earned it over the objections of older and more experienced men. People scrutinized her performance all day hoping for her to make a mistake or show a sign of weakness. She would never willingly give it up. He had a similar problem. She is committed to her job. His career was rooted in Gaborone. Like Sanderson, he'd achieved his success by dint of hard work, long hours, and self sacrifice. And like Sanderson, he'd earned his promotion over the objections of older, wiser, and more experienced men. He couldn't walk away from what he'd worked so hard to attain. So, where would they settle, Gaborone or Kasane?

To be objective, he had no family and was more flexible, could move more easily but, commuting to Kasane from Gaborone was not an option. He could request a transfer north. Well, theoretically, he could. To do so would most likely mean a reduction in rank, a step backward in his career, and possibly put an end to any future advancement. Also, it would mean working under Superintendent Mwambe. That did not strike him as workable. Sanderson, on the other hand, had grown children. Hers might be an empty nest, at the moment, but children, even when they have moved away are like flames to moths and pull on their mothers, and then there is the inevitability of grandchildren. Unless or until Michael and Mpitle settled in Gabz, she would want to be near them, Michael especially. He had nearly died and she had nursed him all those long months. Also, he could relapse at any moment and even with a girlfriend or wife, if that should happen, Sanderson would insist she be there for him. She had nursed and prayed for him before. She would again if she had to. So, would she, could she leave her son in Kasane and move to Gaborone? Not very likely. Yes, Michael was a grown man, but she was his mother and mothers do not recognize that their children are all grown up and no longer need their advice and constant presence.

What to do?

Sanderson swept into the restaurant and for the moment, all of his thoughts of the future evaporated. There would be time to sort this out later. Just now, he wanted only to sit with her and bask in her smile.

"Are you ill, Modise?"

"What? Am I ill? Why are you asking me that?"

"You had a look on your face like you had been too close to the cooking gas and were about to pass out."

"I was thinking of you."

"I make you look like you are going to drop dead from the gas. This is the start to our romantic lunch?"

"Sometimes, Sanderson, you go too far. I was having serious thoughts about you, about us, about…things like that. You come in here and boom, I am wondering if I have wasted my brain on the subject."

"You were thinking about us. You did say *us*?"

"You and me, us, yes. Am I wrong to do that? If so, we will have the waiter and the menus and do our lunch."

"I am sorry, Kgabo. I am…what am I? Not used to this business of dating, and private time alone, and, well, you know."

"You are forgiven. Now, what do you suggest we drink as an antidote to the gas that has nearly killed me?"

Chapter Twenty-five

Danger Woman arrived at the river and settled in a clump of brush where her tawny and spotted pelt made her almost invisible. The sun stood at its zenith. Most of the larger animals would come to the river in the cool of the evening. Smaller ones, those who were prey to the larger ones would arrive when the circumstances for drinking were less dangerous. During the heat of the day, the big cats would stretch out in the park half asleep, the object of tourist oohs and aahs and their incessant picture-taking. The crocodiles would bask half asleep on the riverbank. The bush would be as close to peaceful as it ever got. Smaller animals, whose continued existence depended on their ability to avoid predators, would move about at this time of day in relatively safety. Because their hunters were mostly inert, it meant they did not have to compete for a place at the bank either, where they could otherwise be easily taken.

Danger Woman had learned this along with myriad other useful things about the creatures she and her pack relied on for sustenance. She would wait. A red lechwe, or maybe an aging Thompson's gazelle, separated from its herd, would wander in. At some point, these older animals seemed to be inviting death. If Danger Woman had reasoning powers, she might have ascribed this as a "death wish." As it was, she only saw an opportunity for a quick kill and to eat and then return to her cubs.

A flock of guinea fowl pecked their way across the area between her and the river. She made a dash at them. They squawked and fluttered away. She returned to her lurk and continued her waiting.

Ole caught all this with his camera. He marveled at what he would later call Kotsi Mosadi's intelligence. He knew that intelligence did not really apply to what she'd done. He knew that the hyena had learned from experience what worked and what didn't. The fact she had become the Dominant in the pack meant she had been a quicker learner than her rivals. But shooing off the guinea fowl came close to what in a human world would be considered reasoning. The fowl, if allowed to stay in the interval between her and the river, would function as an alarm that would frighten off any possible victim she might attempt to take down. The clucking and squawking they would make as she made her dash to the river would be more than enough to bring up the heads of her potential prey and warn them of danger. They would be bounding away before she managed to cover half the distance to them. Very smart was Danger Woman, this Kotsi Mosadi.

Ole settled in to wait as well.

Greshenko unfurled the latest note sent by Modise via the game ranger's pen. He glanced at its contents. There was no mention of his request for a clarification of his status, should he survive this business. Modise was in no position to respond. He did note that the director was a man of his word and that would have to be enough. The next paragraph laid out his plans for the next phase of the operation. Greshenko allowed himself an eye-roll at *operation*. Chinese fire drill, more like. Modise wanted to provoke the real Bratva into making a move. He had a plan. It seemed risky to Yuri but he decided to put it to the six men Leo had imported to pose as thugs. They were less seasoned and more likely to take chances than Yuri. He gathered them together and outlined what Modise wanted them to do and what he would do as preparation. All of the men grinned like boy scouts who'd been promised a chance to free-climb El Capitan. They did not seem to grasp, had no concept of the danger involved. That might work to their advantage. If they had any idea what might happen to them if they screwed up, they'd hesitate at the wrong moment and someone would die.

Greshenko went outside and lowered the blue, black, and white of the Botswana flag, inspected its grommets and, assured they would hold, raised it again. Modise happened to be sitting in an unmarked car down the road. He smiled, nodded, and drove away. His next stop was the Mowana Lodge.

◇◇◇

That afternoon two men attired in black suits, white shirts, and black neckties arrived at the Mowana and had a lengthy conversation in the manager's office. Afterwards, one of the men took a position by the entry where he monitored the comings and goings of the lodge's guests. In the meantime, another man went to the unit occupied by Oleg Lenka and his woman and knocked on the door. A man, not Lenka, answered.

"Yes?"

"I would like to speak to Rra Lenka, please."

"Not here. What's this about?"

"It is for Rra Lenka to hear."

Irena Davidova appeared over the man's shoulder. "You can tell me and I will tell Mr. Lenka."

"You are his *nyatse*…ah…his old lady?"

"Old lady? I am his partner, yes. Be careful who you call old."

"Partner, ah. Very well, I must ask you to leave the Mowana Lodge. I am assured that the Marina Lodge down the road has a place suitable for you, but you may not stay here any longer."

"What? Who says this?"

"I am the manager, Missus. It is my duty to tell you this."

"And if we refuse?"

"That is not an option."

Irena peered past the hotel manager's shoulder. At the far end of the hallway she could just make out a man in a black suit, white shirt, and black tie. He smiled, raised his hand, and waved goodbye. She slammed the door in the manager's face.

Cszepanski called Lenka with the news of the lodge's decision to terminate their stay. Lenka rushed back to the hotel and had Irena repeat what the manager said. He called the manager's office and heard the same thing. He was to vacate by noon the following day. So sorry but…Lenka called his two best men and instructed them to scour the hotel and take care of the man or men in black suits. No one would push him out. How dare they muscle in to what he'd considered his territory? Irena said she had told him to move and that if he didn't, Greshenko would take over the protection business, and now he had. Lenka told her to shut the hell up. Cszepanski left. Things were either unraveling or the war had begun and in either case, he wanted to be better positioned.

Lenka's men arrived and scoured the premises. The only unattached European men they found were lounging at the bar sharing a pitcher of Manhattans. They were wearing Hawaiian shirts, not black suits. Their trousers were black, though. They asked if one of Lenka's people was their guide. They said they had hired a private guide for a safari. The men left them in the bar without answering their question. Had they turned, they might have seen the smirk on the face of the larger one.

Lenka ordered his people to take up a post at the entrance and watch everyone going in and out. They were to stay there until eleven o'clock and then return at eight the following morning. If Greshenko's man or men, for that is who he assumed they must be, appeared, they were to take care of them.

"Now what?" Lenka asked Irena. "What happened to Cszepanski?"

"He left to organize your men against the possibility you will have a shootout on your hands. Oleg, you hesitated and now this. They have, how you say…the high ground?"

"It was only a trial, a test. They are gone. They are not really here, you see? You heard. Those men left the premises. Greshenko is playing games. He is pushing to see what we will do. Well, I know how to play games, too. He will be sorry."

Irena rolled her eyes and left the room. She also had some planning of her own to do.

Lenka's men posted at the entrance to the lodge spent the remainder of the day watching guests coming and going. A few smiled at them and said *Dumela*. They nodded in return. But for most of the day they stood shifting their weight from one foot to another. Boredom overtook them, as did the heat. Speculation about the sexual proclivities of the boss' woman took the edge off the first problem. Chilled beer eased the second.

Chapter Twenty-six

Danger Woman crouched unmoving in her lurk. An hour passed and finally a warthog with three offspring trotted down to the river. The female nosed her newborns into some nearby brush and slipped to the river to drink. Danger Woman had a choice to make. One or two of the piglets or the mother? She chose the former. She could easily carry off two of them in her mouth and their mother would not attempt to pursue for fear of losing her only surviving offspring. Danger Woman crawled on her belly to the bush, snatched one small warthog, and with one sharp shake broke its neck. She dropped it before either of the remaining two could bolt. She snatched a second, worked it back in her jaws, snapped up the first, and trotted off to the south with the two baby warthogs firmly in her jaws before the female at the river realized what had happened.

The guinea fowl returned. Too late.

Boredom had finally taken its toll on Lenka's men. They grew careless. Their attention wandered. By ten o'clock it was all they could do to stay on their feet. They rubbed their eyes, slipped off their shoes and wriggled their toes. Eleven could not come soon enough. Lenka had not seen fit to relieve them, so they remained at the entrance, weary and annoyed. They did so, that is, until two men in black suits and white shirts sidled up behind them and produced large automatics. The men poked them in the back with the barrels of the pistols and suggested they move away from the hotel. They marched a hundred meters down the road and were told to stop. They were quickly disarmed, their hands were zip-tied behind their backs, and a sack pulled over their heads. Blinded and unable to even feel their way along, they stumbled forward and were unceremoniously shoved into a van. The door slammed shut and they were driven off, they knew not where.

Forty-five minutes later, and after being driven over bumpy roads with the direction constantly changed, the van braked. The van door screeched open. Hands dragged them out and stood them up. Hands grasping their elbows forced them to stumble forward ten meters or so. They heard a thump as if a heavy object had been dropped nearby. The zip-ties were cut from their wrists and they were knocked off their feet. They fumbled the knots loose and removed the bags from their heads. The sound of a vehicle jolting off and growing fainter in the distance constituted all they knew of their captors. They were alone in the darkness.

A slight breeze carried the odor of fear into the bush. Animals scattered by the noise of the van, turned and pricked up their ears. Predators tensed and tasted the air. Somewhere, not too far from them, a candidate for killing had appeared. A leopard slithered down from the branches of a nearby tree. She chirped to call her two cubs. It was time for them to learn the intricacies of the hunt. The three of them crept toward the promise of a meal, a large one. There were no lions in the area and the hyenas were not hunting as a pack. That meant that the field was open to the leopard. She lifted her head to see where her prey was located. Her cubs imitated her and followed suit. Six eyes locked on the two men and tracked their every move.

"Where are we?" the one who answered to Georgei asked.

"Be damned if I know." He took a breath and caught the rank smell of heavy foliage. "It looks like a forest."

Somewhere in the distance they heard an elephant trumpet.

"By Christ, we're in the damned park. They brought us out here to feed the damned animals."

They stared frantically into the darkness searching for feral yellow-green eyes, listening for the stealthy approach of a big cat. Lions, leopards, even hyenas could leap on them and they'd disappear forever. Just as real panic was about to set in, lights, headlights, flashed at them from down the track. They waved and shouted at whoever was in the vehicle. Anybody was better than being lost and unarmed in the game park at night. The vehicle pulled up in front of them. Someone barked orders and a group of men dismounted from what they now realized was a large truck. A truck painted olive drab, a truck full of men from the Botswana Defense Force, the BDF. One of the men who seemed to have officer's flashes on his shoulder stepped up to them.

"So, gentlemen, can you tell me what you two are doing in the park in the middle of the night?" This must be the man in charge.

Relieved the men grinned and raised their hands to their waist, palms up. "Right. Look, Captain, we are the victims here. See, about an hour ago, some guys stuck guns in our back and we were forced into this van thing and driven out here. They were...ah, criminals, right? And they tied us up and drove us out here and dumped us to be killed by the lions or something. Thank God you found us."

"It's lieutenant, Lieutenant Mosekisi, not captain. So, you are telling me that you were kidnapped, driven here, by...you did say criminals, correct? And then you think you were to perish with no means of escape?"

"Exactly. Thank God you happened to drive by. Get us out of here."

"There is something you need to know before you say anything else. We did not happen to drive by. As to getting you out of here, I assure you that is precisely what we will do. But first, how will you explain that *bakkie* over there? It is at a taxi stand, maybe?"

"Bocky? What the hell is a bocky?

"That truck over there. It is not yours?"

They spun around and saw a pickup parked ten meters away. They recognized it as one of Lenka's.

"That's not ours, exactly. I mean it is but, we didn't know it was there."

"I see. You are standing here in the middle of the game park with your truck but you forgot it was there? No? Do you have a key for this *bakkie's* ignition?"

"Key? No, of course not. We didn't know—"

"You didn't know it sat there, yes, so you said. It's bigger than a water buffalo and still you say you didn't know it was there. Corporal, search these men's pockets."

"Hey, wait a minute. Listen you probably don't realize who you are dealing with here. Do you recognize the name Lenka?"

"No. Corporal, you found something?"

"This one has a key that will most likely fit that *Bakkie's* ignition slot, for sure."

"Someone put it there. It's not mine."

"Of course they did. These bad men, these criminals, as you say, kidnapped you, left you for dead in the middle of the game park and then slipped a key to a truck which is 'not exactly' yours, and left you to die. That is your story. Yes, I understand. You are the victims. Now, can you tell me what is in this bag here on the ground?"

"Bag? What bag?"

The officer in charge shook his head and nudged a lumpy bag at their feet with his boot. "This one."

"Never saw it before in my life."

"Like the key to the truck, yes? Sergeant, bring the canvas sheet and spread it out here. Now sirs, would you please empty your bag on the canvas?"

"Our bag? I already told you, it's not…never mind. Empty it? Okay. The first man picked up the bag and the second untied the knot at its mouth. They tipped the bag over and several large objects tumbled out.

While the sergeant focused his flashlight on the contents, the lieutenant fixed the two men with a look that had cowed recruits for the last year and a half. "Can you identify these things?"

"Beats the hell out of me. What are they?"

"Playing the fool will not help you. You know very well that these are rhinoceros horns. As I said before, we did not just happen to drive out here. We received a tip that there were poachers at work and here you are. So, it appears we have caught ourselves those very poachers. You know that poaching is a serious crime in Botswana. We in this country are not very fond of poachers. Perhaps you have heard that? No? Well, to be clear, we treat them with fairness and then throw the book at them. That is the expression, no? Throw the book?"

"*Kristus.* We aren't poachers. Jesus, look around you. If we was poachers, where is the dead rhinos?"

"Deeper in the park, I judge, attracting all sorts of scavengers and other meat eaters. Under those circumstances, I doubt you would not be so foolish to stay with the carcass. What I don't understand is why are you standing here at all?"

"What?"

"A sensible poacher will make his kill, harvest what he wants, and leave as quickly and as quietly as possible, but you are standing here in the middle of the park waiting. Waiting for what? Or is it who? Ah, I see. You were expecting to meet your buyer. I presume it to be someone trading with the Chinese, no doubt. Yes, yes. Well, they will not be buying any rhinoceros horns tonight. Corporal, cuff these men. Put a man in that truck of theirs. We will take these men and their horns to headquarters."

"We get a lawyer, a solicitor, don't we?"

"As I told you before poaching is a serious crime. You will be lucky to get a trial."

"But we were framed."

The members of the BDF grabbed the men by the arms and began to frog march them toward the truck.

"Of course you were. As you said, you were bound and driven to the park and set down with a bag of contraband by people you cannot identify and who disappeared but left you a truck which you say is not yours, but is somehow."

"But, we were."

"You wish us to believe this fairy tale? You do realize how difficult that would be for someone to do all that to two able-bodied men like yourselves and not leave a mark? But just look at you, hardly mussed. Oh, yes, maybe it was an alien from outer space that killed the rhinos and then beamed you and your *bakkie* into the park. A very elaborate frame, I'm thinking. I also believe you have been reading too many American mystery books and watching their television. My ten-year-old son could dream up a better story. Very well, Corporal, put them in the truck."

Kgabo Modise held the rank of captain in the BDF Reserve. In uniform and with the permission from the Company commander, he'd joined the foray into the park and had watched the scene unfold before him. It was he who had called for the raid in the first place and he wanted to see it to completion. No, these two thugs were not going to see blue sky until long after Lenka and his people were sent far away.

The leopard sat back on her haunches. The noise and confusion were too much for her. She rose and led her cubs away. There would be game closer to the river. She would take them there.

Chapter Twenty-seven

Lenka awakened to loud knocking at his door. He rolled over and realized there was no one else in the bed. He sat up. Irena's voice cut through the air. It was the tone she used when she had reached that level of anger when Lenka would say her voice could etch glass. Something had happened. He pulled on a robe and went to the door. Irena, wearing not much more than a scowl stood, arms akimbo, screaming in Russian at the manager who stood, open-mouthed and uncomprehending.

"What is this?" Oleg said.

"He is giving us a bill and saying we must vacate, is what."

"I thought I told you yesterday that we were not leaving. You said there were men who threatened you. So, they are gone. There are no men. We are done here. My men are at the entrance and you will not be bothered by those other people anymore and you will not bother me."

Lenka moved to shut the door but the hotel manager managed to put a hand out and stopped it.

"Your people are not standing at my entrance. Those men who wish to control this hotel are there. Now please understand. They said there could be accidents, a fire, or worse. You must leave. I will send a bellman up with a cart." He turned and left.

Lenka dressed in shirt, trousers, and slippers and dashed to the front entrance. Two men, not the same two as the day before, but dressed in the same black suits and white shirts, stood at the front of the hotel.

One of them waved and smiled. "Your guys are gone. Said they'd had enough of Africa. Do you need help with your bags?"

Lenka reached into his waistband for the gun that was not there. Had it been, had he paused to complete his dressing, there would have been some serious bloodshed at the Mowana Lodge that morning. When he realized it wasn't tucked into his belt and looked up, he faced two men with significant firepower aimed at his forehead. He retreated back into the hotel and called Cszepanski.

"Where are Georgei and Josif? They were told to be at this hotel."

"No one has heard from them or seen them since they went to the hotel last night. I have asked our sources. They are not under arrest locally. They are gone."

Lenka hung up. He finished dressing, including his gun, yelled at Irena to move her ass, and went out the front door. There was no sign of the manager, but the two men were still standing outside. They grinned and waved.

"Moving yet? Let us know if you need help."

Irena followed him out the door and they said something lewd in Russian to her.

"You," she said to one of them, "you are from Ukraine? You have that accent."

"Chicago," he answered. "Say, sweetheart, it's okay with us if you stay. We just want your ugly boyfriend gone, see?"

"Not happening, Sonny. This is Oleg Lenka. He eats pretty boys like you for breakfast."

"Sure he does and I will lose a lot of sleep thinking about that. Say, what happened to the two morons who were here last night? They decide to not report for duty this morning? Maybe we scared them off. You think we might have? Or, they figured that mister Tough Guy here wasn't tough enough? Maybe they decided to find employment elsewhere. What do you think, Tough Guy? Did your boys run home to momma, did they sign on with the real thing, or just run for cover?"

Lenka reached for his gun. Irena put a hand on his. "Not now, Oleg. Not now. We go."

"Not now, Oleg, not now, we go," the two men sang in a falsetto and waved him away to the parking lot.

"We go to Greshenko and settle this," he said. "I am calling Cszepanski and telling him to bring the men to the casino. We will see who is what."

Lenka and a second SUV arrived at the casino at the same time as two truckloads of BDF forces. The soldiers formed a cordon around the casino. Lenka pulled to the side of the road, unsure what to do next. Cszepanski hopped out of the SUV and tapped on Lenka's window. Lenka lowered it.

"What?"

"Our guy inside called just now. They are looking for the people who are responsible for two poachers they caught last night."

"Poachers? So, Greshenko is poaching, too?"

"Not sure about that. Just that our guy says two men were caught and one mentioned a name. Since it sounded Russian, they naturally thought it must be Greshenko. He is the local Russian, you could say. Chief, you might be next, if they clear him."

"Me? I don't know anything about poaching. How long are they going to stay?"

"No idea, but we look pretty obvious sitting here. Maybe we should head back to the warehouse and rethink this."

"Nothing to rethink, Cszepanski. I am going to kill that man and his smart ass associates."

"But not today." Irena said. "We go to the warehouse, like Cszepanski says. We need to arrange a few things first. Nobody is getting shot today."

Modise took up a position inside the casino at a window. He had field glasses trained on the car and SUV across the road. Would Lenka dare to approach the building even with the BDF there? He didn't think Lenka was that stupid, but he hoped he might be. He was disappointed but not surprised when the two vehicles made a U-turn and drove away.

"They will go to their warehouse headquarters and regroup," said Greshenko, who had been watching over his shoulder.

"And then what?"

"They will wait for the BDF to leave and nightfall. Then they will return. They will not be in a mood to negotiate, I don't think."

"In that case, I think it is time you were arrested for something or another and your 'men' brought in for questioning."

"That is only a stalling tactic, Modise. Sooner or later, you are going to have to let the confrontation between us take place. When you do, people will be killed. It is what has been set in motion the minute you bought into Leo's plan. You had to know that."

"I assumed it, yes, but remember the plan never called for the use of the BDF and if I have my way, nobody dies."

"Good luck with that. So, now what will you and the BDF do?"

"They will do nothing. I cannot put them in harm's way and not expect everyone from the President on down not to come after me. No, they were for one night and one day only. I am the exception and they have loaned me a truck. It will be driving about and constantly in the way of whatever those people do. They do not need to know that there are no BDF forces in the back or driving it."

"So, I ask you again, what comes next?"

"I think we take you away for awhile and ask your people to step down. I don't really want Lenka out of the hotel where he is staying, only harassed from time to time. Your men will disappear from the Mowana Lodge as they did before. Then when he thinks he's won, they will return if necessary. I want him off balance. After a while his temper will get the better of him and he will do something stupid and then we will have him on a plane to Russia."

"Not Russia, Inspector, South Africa. He is settled in Cape Town. You will have to persuade the South Africans to deport him as well."

"We are working on that. I know that some of their officials are easily bought, but even on a bad day, they can only manage to overlook so much thuggery and Lenka is a latecomer to their system. The entrenched Bratva will see to it he is not allowed to compete."

"I hope you're right. I'd feel better if there was some kind of permanent solution, Inspector. The Bratva is like mold in your house. Once it gets in it is impossible to get out, except maybe to burn down the house. I don't want you to have your house burn down, Modise."

Chapter Twenty-eight

Danger Woman had managed to leave her lair and return on two occasions without incident. No other hyenas intent on removing her from her position as pack dominant had made an attempt to displace her. No lions with murderous intentions of their own had laid in wait for her. Nothing. She had eaten and fed her pups. They were thriving. In another day or two she would let them out into the fresh air. Hunting had been easy. Today, she'd managed to drag back a significant portion of the haunch from a small gazelle that a leopard had brought down, but had dropped from the tree that served as her lurk. Before the leopard followed her kill to the ground to retrieve it, Kotsi Mosadi had been able to dash in and snatch the haunch. The leopard chased her for a few meters and then doubled back, lest some other scavenger take the remainder of the gazelle or attack her cubs. Now, Kotsi Mosadi lolled at the entrance of her dugout and sampled the air for danger. She sensed none. For Danger Woman life was good.

She acknowledged the presence of Ole Andersen's Land Rover only to the extent that she had become accustomed to it. It had never required her or her pack to vary their routine. At first they were wary of the great thing but after a while it held no more fear for them than a tree or an elephant. In the bush, nothing could be counted on as an absolute.

◇◇◇

Ole Andersen noted the hyena's purloined meal. "Kleptoparasitism," he muttered and thought of his sponsors enjoying a leisurely luncheon back at their lodge. The things one had to do to keep a career alive. He turned his attention back to his obsession, Danger Woman. Ole had been happy to discover that the late night horn blowing he'd been forced to do when he'd spotted the human skull had not permanently altered his favored position with Danger Woman and her pack. So, as Danger Woman fed her cubs and then took the air, his camera kept on capturing the life cycle of one of the world's least loved animals. Occasionally he stooped to look through its eyepiece to check on the focus and field.

He wondered if by intruding on the life of this animal, he might somehow be altering her behavior in a significant way. It would be a difference he could not measure. Did Heisenberg's Uncertainty Principle apply to wildlife chroniclers? It was a thought, probably not a complete one, and it did violence to Heisenberg's intent if Ole understood anything about quantum mechanics, which he admitted he did not. Still, he felt it must have some merit. Surely, a great, noisy Land Rover parked in the pathway of a hunting pack must somehow influence their behavior one way or the other. What if it inhibited shyer species from approaching? Wouldn't that alter what was hunted or the competition? A leopard, for example, in the absence of humankind in the form of an SUV, might compete with the hyena and the consequences of the hunt might be changed significantly. Not for the killed animal, of course. Ole would think about to what extent his constant presence changed the way this pack behaved over and against what it might have done had he and his Land Rover not been around. Perhaps he would write a paper about it. A science academy would be interested in the topic, surely.

A light breeze rustled the bush. Not much of a breeze, just enough to stir the smaller leaves on trees and brush. It came from the north this afternoon. Because of that, neither he nor Danger Woman were aware that the lions had returned and had both of them in sight. The lions held a different view of Ole's truck than Danger Woman. For the lions, it represented an opportunity, the possibility of a quick kill. If the contents of the thing were to step from it or even make themselves vulnerable, they would pounce. To be dragged from a vehicle is not as rare an occurrence in this part of the world as some might be led to believe. Ole knew that. He also thought he had made the proper adjustments to his vehicle. The doors closed tightly and locked. The steel mesh on the windows he tested once a week to be sure it would withstand any attempt by a quarter-ton lion might make to tear them away. And he kept a close watch of his immediate surroundings. At least most of the time he did. Today his attention stayed focused on the burrow and Danger Woman's possible exit.

It almost cost him his life. Between his focus on Danger Woman and his daydreaming about Heisenberg, he did not hear the lioness pad up to the rear of his vehicle and had he not turned his head marginally he would not have caught sight of her readying to leap onto the truck. As it happened, he did, and managed to drop down into the truck along with the camera and slam the roof hatch shut before the lion completed the maneuver. She relaxed from her crouch and attacked the side of the truck with her paws. Ole started the motor and backed away. He knew that if the lion managed to attract the attention of other members of the pride and between them they were to get the right purchase on the side of the truck, it might flip it on its side. At that point Ole would have been trapped like a caged animal. The irony would not be lost on him. Further he would have to hope help would arrive before the lions figured how to break into the cab.

Some years ago he had lost a colleague who went to Australia to study sharks and had been in a shark cage that could withstand the efforts of a single great white, but not a half dozen. Ole shifted gears and drove from the area as quickly as the road allowed. The lioness trotted after him for twenty meters or so and then wheeled around and turned back. He wondered if she really thought he could be taken or if she had merely wanted to establish her territory.

Ole mopped his brow and thanked his lucky stars. If he hadn't glanced over his shoulder when he did, things could have gotten messy.

Danger Woman had disappeared.

Cszepanski thought he saw the writing on the wall. This operation teetered on the brink. To restore it meant all-out war on Greshenko's gang. He wondered if Lenka would be up for that. He had had it easy in St. Petersburg, if the rumors were true. Would he have the stones to face off with the real thing? Also troubling him was the presence of the soldiers, the BDF. They presented a different set of problems. Did anyone really want to go to war with the local army? How did they fit in with this business? He'd never had to confront an army.

Actually, that wasn't completely true. The only other time he'd been involved in an attempt to control a portion of another country had been in Bosnia a very long time ago. He'd been very young, trailing along at the heels of a man he thought invincible. The military had inserted itself into that operation. It had not been pretty. He was alive today only because they thought it not worth the trouble to chase after a ten-year-old when he bolted out the door. Everyone else had been bagged and shot. He never forgot what happened that day. Remembering it made him wonder about what hornet's nest Lenka had kicked over. He started to map out his exit strategy just in case he needed one, and he thought he did.

Lenka and the Davidova arrived. By the look of them, they had had words on the way to the warehouse. Lenka ordered the men to wait outside while the three of them talked. Cszepanski flipped the safety off on his Beretta. Irena removed her compact and laid down a line of coke which she inhaled. Her eyes brightened. A bad sign, Cszepanski thought. There will be fireworks before this day is over. He hoped the woman had enough control to wait until Lenka had shot his wad before she started yapping. He knew she was the brains in the organization. He also knew that Lenka didn't admit to that and if she pushed him too hard, too soon, things could get messy for her and for everyone else.

He would stay quiet and see how this played out.

Chapter Twenty-nine

Irena spoke first. "So, Oleg, what happens now? We are no closer to having Greshenko than we were a week ago."

"What happens now is for you to shut up and stay that way. Cszepanski, how many men do we have available to go over there and finish this?"

"Here? Do you want to know many we have, or how many can we count on if there is shooting?"

"What? We have people who will not fight?"

"Chief, we have men and women placed in the hotels. They are spies, I guess you could call them. They are not guns. They are hired help, not for the trenches. The men we have who were signed to provide guns are fewer, nine in all. That includes the two Boers. I have my doubts about them. So, the safe bet is seven."

"I thought I told you to bring everyone up here."

"Chief, I made the call. Then I got to thinking about it. That is exactly what they want—to have us all in one place so they can take us all out at the same time. I told them to wait, but, in terms of guns, if they came, it would only add two. The others are technical. They are the last people we want here. If it comes to a face off, we have what we need. I don't know what Greshenko has exactly, but our man inside says there are only seven, counting Greshenko."

"But I told you I wanted them here." Lenka's face had become beet red.

"Listen to him, Oleg," Irena said. She handed him a glass of vodka with a few ice chips in it.

"And I told you to shut up. You said seven. How is that possible? How can he mount such a thing with seven?"

"Hear me out, Boss. First, I am not sure it is Greshenko who is after us. It seems like it and then, I don't know, things don't make sense. Like, this afternoon, before you called, but after you left the hotel, I drove by to see for myself who was at the entrance."

"And you saw Greshenko's men."

Cszepanski shook his head and lit one of his Turkish cigarettes. "No, I didn't see anyone. So, I go in and talk to the manager and I ask him, just as a matter of curiosity, see? Why you are asking Mr. Lenka to leave. I told him I was a business associate of yours and planned a conference at a hotel and his was my first choice. But, I said, if Mr. Lenka could not stay in his hotel, I doubted I would book it."

"And?"

"And he shrugged and claimed he didn't know what I was talking about. He said he had no record of a request having been made to have you removed."

"What? The slimy little... He stood there and told me to my face that I had to leave. He knows who I am and what I can do and he tells me this anyway."

"What did this manager who spoke to you look like?"

"Look like? Little pipsqueak of a man. Stupid little moustache and a lisp."

"That's it. He isn't little. He is a big black man. He could have been an American footballer."

"No, that's wrong. The manager is a short brown man with a moustache and very black hair. He sounded like those people from India or Pakistan, like that."

"Tall, big, bald, and dark. He showed me his ID. He was the manager, alright. Chief, we're being played. It looks like Greshenko is trying to set us up. And then, there is the army."

"What about the army? They are after poachers. They think Greshenko is hiring them."

"See, that is the second thing that doesn't work. Why would he be poaching? That is the single most dangerous thing someone in his position could possibly do. Here is my problem with the soldiers. It is from a personal experience, okay? Okay. In the past I have seen that when they are in the area, in the action, so to speak, it means one of two things, they are involved or they are being used. I think Greshenko faked that poaching story to draw them in and to scare us off. If not, then I think we need to leave because if the army is in his pocket, we are cooked."

"That can't be. This country is nearly incorruptible that way. The President is a general, for God's sake."

"He was a general. Not anymore," Irena murmured.

"I told you to shut up. I'm saying this has to be something else. I think all we need to do is wait until they clear out and then go over to that casino and shoot every one of them."

Irena threw up her hands and shouted at Lenka. "And we will be in jail by breakfast. First we need to figure out what the game is here. Who is doing this to us?"

"I said for you…It is Greshenko. That's it. Does anyone not hear that? So, one at a time as before. Pick them off, take them to the river or the bush and feed the animals. It is what got us this far. We stay on the plan." Lenka sat down heavily at the desk and began to open and close its drawers. "Where is that nine millimeter that was in here?"

Cszepanski shrugged. "I think one of the Boers took it. They sell them to the locals. I'll talk to them tomorrow."

"Do that. What are we hearing from the cloned phone?"

"That's another thing that is screwy. We are hearing too much."

"What do you mean 'too much'? How can too much be a bad thing?"

"They are talking all the time. Who does that? Worse, what they are babbling about doesn't match with what we know from our sources on the ground."

"Like what?"

"They talk about the progress of operations with crazy names. They say smuggling is being done. We have had nothing coming in or out for days and as far as I know, no one else has either. Why are they saying this? In my experience, Boss, police don't talk so much on the phone. They say things like, we have to be here or we have to be there. There is a situation, call for backup, that sort of thing or words that are coded and then the details they give at meetings, you know? I expect to hear a brief word or a request. Not what these people go on about. Also, why are they talking so much in the open? If I were mounting a drive against you, I sure as hell would be using an encrypted phone."

"So, they are not so smart as us and is a new country. They are like children learning to run a country like children playing house. They don't know, Cszepanski, how civilization works. That is something we will teach them."

"Maybe, but I don't think so. It is a big mistake to under-estimate them. You take that Modise guy, he is no dummy."

Irena risked being snapped at again and broke in. "He has a girlfriend, yes? The game ranger is the one. If Modise is a problem, we take her out of play and if he has any regard for her he will back down. That is Bratva way."

Lenka started to say something and then thought better of it.

"It is a possibility. She should be easy enough to pick up." Cszepanski said.

Irena sensing Lenka had calmed sufficiently, said, "In St. Petersburg, we had canals and ice, here it is river and park. Not so different. Think about it, Oleg, not such a big deal. Okay, now we should go to hotel, take shower, and sleep. Tomorrow we plan how, and when, and who goes first for a swim with the crocodiles, okay?"

"Okay. Tomorrow we will start removing those men from the area. When there is only Greshenko...he is mine."

Chapter Thirty

Sanderson awoke with in a panic. Her heart pounded like she had run a race with a cheetah and lost. She could feel the pulse in her neck without touching it. She fumbled to switch on the light, nearly knocked the lamp over, caught it before it crashed to the floor and managed to get it lit. She looked at her clock. It read 22:00 hours. That might not be inordinately late by many people's standards but, for a game ranger whose day began at dawn or near to, ten o'clock at night is like three in the morning. She swung her legs over the edge and sat on the side of the bed. She took several deep breaths. Her heart slowed to near normal. She sipped some water from a glass on the bedside table and wiped her brow.

What had made her jump out of sleep like that? Her grandmother would have said the "crocodiles had eaten her soul." Sanderson never understood what she meant by that. She assumed it had something to do with premonitions or fear of the unknown or that someone had her on their mind and not in a nice way. She had plenty of unknowns popping up in her life at the moment. Kgabo Modise, for one. Where did she believe that relationship would go? So much separated them, geography chief among them. Should she have doubts or fear about Kgabo and her possible future with him? Also, those Lenka men could easily shoot him dead. What then? Policemen live dangerous lives. Being made a widow a second time didn't sound like something she would like to go through again. And he lived in Gaborone. Would she move? Would he? What was she thinking? Modise had never said anything about marriage, had he? He hinted at lunch that he spent time thinking about *us,* didn't he? So what did that mean?

Michael and Mpitle had to be considered, didn't they? Would Michael's HAART last or would his AIDs force him to return to his bed? She had stopped reading about his disease when he suddenly lost the symptoms and returned to health. What happens if the clock stops and then marches backward? And Mpitle is so far away. She missed her daughter the most. When she believed that Michael would die, she had grown calluses on her brain about that and had turned to Mpitle. Now what?

Nagging at the back of her mind, however, was the thought that quite possibly her grandmother's "crocodile" was not after Modise, or Mpitle, or Michael, but it was coming for her. Some very bad person had her, Game Ranger Sanderson, on his mind and it had nothing to do with nice things, no.

Hours would pass before she drifted off to sleep again.

Mpitle's new roommate was a mystery. She said she had classes to attend but, every time Mpitle turned around, there she was. Sometimes she read a book or tapped away at her tablet. Sometimes she talked on her mobile phone and sometimes she just stared at it and then at the surroundings. It seemed very strange. She doused her light. Kopano's remained on as she surfed the web on her iPad.

"Every time I turn about, there you are, Kopano. Don't you ever go to class?"

"Oh yes, of course I do. But you see my classes are either tutorials or on-line. For the tutorials, I meet with my instructor for a short time and then I go about my day. Almost everything I need, I have downloaded onto my tablet. So, I find a nice place to sit and do my work there. Technology is changing education in many wonderful ways, don't you think?"

"So this is how graduate work is pursued?"

"Definitely."

"I think I will like graduate studies better than these under-graduate ones, for sure."

"I'm sure you will. Good night, Mpitle."

Irena managed to bring Lenka back to center. It hadn't been hard. It never was. A few slipped buttons, whispered suggestions, and he became as docile as a newborn. Actually, she didn't know if that was the case. She had no experience with newborns. Her life on the street, forced on her at an unacceptably young age, had removed any possibilities in that department. Lenka slept and she watched.

When he reached the point in his snoring she recognized as the moment of deep sleep, she rose and began her post-coital routine. She emptied his pockets of change and bills. The larger denominations she counted, reduced the stack by thirty percent, and placed the remainder on the dresser for him to find along with the coins. She checked his notebook and memorized any new numbers he had written down. His mind worked like a sieve when it came to details so he wrote things he thought important down in his book. Some of the numbers were for bank accounts; some were phone numbers with St. Petersburg area codes. They might be useful. Most of them she already knew by heart, but maintaining this routine strengthened her ability to recall them if and when she would need them.

She removed his nine millimeter from its holster, dropped the clip and ejected the shell from the chamber. It was a precaution she always followed since the night in St. Petersburg when he'd been roused from deep sleep by a backfire, or perhaps it had been an actual gunshot. In any event, he rolled to the floor and come to a crouch firing his pistol at anything that moved. He'd nearly blown her head off. Lenka had issues that even she could not erase. So, she unloaded the gun.

There did not appear to be anything else of interest in his pockets or his briefcase. She tucked the stolen bills in the secret compartment in her purse with the previous day's haul and surveyed the room. Satisfied she hadn't overlooked anything, she slipped a robe over her naked body, turned out the lights, and went out on her balcony.

Time and tide, someone said, waits for no one. She couldn't remember who. Time and tide. She had the impression that her tide and time had caught up with her, were at the point where the process reversed. She realized that for her, time had begun to run out. She needed a plan and whatever she decided to do, it needed to be done in the dark. She knew if Lenka discovered what she had in mind, he'd probably kill her and dump her in the bush with the half dozen others he'd sent there. Not all of them had been dead when they had made the trip to the park. They'd been dumped helpless with their limbs and mouth duct-taped. She shivered at the memory.

Even thinking about being abandoned in the bush at night with ferocious and hungry animals prowling about terrified her. Lenka, she knew, could be managed. Wild animals were another story. The best plan would be for him to die first. Who could she get to kill him? If she were in St. Petersburg, she knew at least a dozen men who would be more than happy to do that for her. Africa is a long ways away from that mostly frozen country. With Grelnikov dead, there was only one person locally who was available, smart enough, and tough enough to do it. But, could she seduce Cszepanski right under Lenka's nose? She poured vodka into a glass and drank it neat. Cszepanski was the sort of man who did not need her help or anyone's help. Perhaps she could put a pillow over Lenka's face and sit on it. Would that work? Lenka might be slow in the brain but he was very strong and fast. He would reach around and toss her across the room and have her in a stranglehold before she bounced. No, killing Lenka wouldn't work. So what to do?

It took three more visits to the vodka bottle before she could finally return to bed and sleep.

◇◇◇

Danger Woman slipped from her lair and this time took a course away from the river. The hunting would be better in the bush.

Hunting by day had been necessary at first and she might have to do it again, but night hunting came naturally to her. Her hunting range could be larger which meant better. The cubs were sufficiently developed and intuitively she knew that she could leave them for longer periods of time now. Even if they left the burrow, they would not wander very far and the darkness would protect them from any predator except the cats. She moved off at a fast trot, sniffing the air and getting her bearings. She made a point to skirt the area her nose told her carried the distinct scent of lion. She paused, listened, and headed south.

Chapter Thirty-one

Joseph Ikanya had doubts. Modise asked him to do something he'd never done before in his life. He expected him to perform actual police work. Well, that didn't quite cover it. He'd been a policeman for two decades and had put in his time in uniform patrolling village streets. But his job for at least fifteen years of those two decades he'd spent sitting behind a desk or attending meetings and issuing policy directives. Traffic control did not involve him in the things people usually think of when they speak of police work. If you needed a parade organized or a diplomat protected, you called on Joseph Ikanya, but gun-toting and confrontations with gangsters, maybe not. Yet, here was Modise asking him to risk his life in this gang war business.

Superintendent Mwambe had warned him about Modise. "Meddler," he'd said. "Always butting his Gaborone nose into local policing." Apparently Mwambe had no equal reservations about Joseph's Gaborone nose. Yet, when Modise had pressed the two of them into service as voices on the phones that were supposedly cloned, both he and Mwambe had enjoyed themselves immensely. It had been exciting to be part of this "sting." Still, it is one thing to play at the business while being well out of the way of any kind of real peril, quite another to be in the middle of what could become a very dangerous situation. He reminded Modise that he would soon be a father and his poor wife would not want him to take such chances. Her condition was very delicate, he'd said.

Ikanya wanted to beg off, and Modise said he understood,

of course. Perhaps he would have to call the director and ask for someone to be sent up to take his place. Joseph worried about that. What if the director asked why he'd refused to participate and Modise said it was because Inspector Ikanya had scruples, had worried about his safety? So there was no avoiding it. He would risk his life. He would perform his duty for his country. He hoped his wife, soon to be his widow, would forgive him.

Modise wanted him to go "undercover." Well, not undercover precisely. He wanted him to pretend to be a bookkeeper at the casino. All he had to do was sit at a desk and if anyone asked where Rra Greshenko was, he was to say he had left for Gaborone, and if they asked about the other men, to say they were going to the Okavango. There were other things he had to be prepared to mention as well. Modise gave him a script to read. He'd said that he was to grasp only the gist of it and then improvise. "It must not sound rehearsed," he'd said. Joseph said he could do that. He had been in the Dramatics Club in the last year of his schooling and he was often asked to be Father Christmas at the church. So, yes, he was prepared, and not only could, but he would do it, he'd said, but not with great conviction.

When he'd agreed to it late the night before, it had all seemed simple. Sit and pretend to be a bookkeeper auditing the casino books. Answer a few questions and they would leave. Modise thought they would head west. At least they would not bother him. When they'd gone, he would be free to return to his room at the government house or continue his contact with Mwambe. Furthermore, Modise said he should not worry. They had planted listening devices in the room and if any trouble started they would break in and arrest them. He would be perfectly safe at all times.

Now, sitting at the desk with the possibility of some murderers dropping by, Joseph was not so sure. His eyes scanned the walls in search of the hidden microphones; he wanted to be absolutely sure he spoke into them.

"Here they come," a voice which seemed to come from the ceiling said. "Get ready and good luck."

Too late to back out now.

>>>

Lenka had risen early. He'd staggered into the shower. His memories of the previous night, that is the last few hours of it, had seemed muddled. Showered and shaved, he'd popped half a dozen aspirins and studied the contents of his closet. The Armani sharkskin fitted best when he wore his shoulder holster. He pulled it off its hanger, donned a black shirt and white tie, slipped on the suit. He always made it a point to be well dressed when he intended to kill someone and today he intended to settle with Greshenko. He'd called Cszepanski and told him to bring the men up to the lodge. They were to be armed and ready. They were going to the casino and finish with Greshenko. He hung up before Cszepanski could respond. Lenka had no interest in hearing one of his cautionary lectures. This time they would do as he was told.

Lenka and his crew arrived in three SUVs. He headed to the casino's offices and pushed through the door. He expected to catch Greshenko by surprise. But the only person in the office was nervous little man in a rumpled suit and wearing an old-fashioned eye shade.

"Where is Greshenko?" he demanded.

"Excuse me?" The little man mopped his forehead.

Lenka grabbed him by the necktie and pulled him forward. "Are you deaf? I asked where is Yuri Greshenko?"

"The executive manager of the casino? That Yuri Greshenko?"

"Are you stupid? There is more than one Yuri Greshenko?"

"I wouldn't know about that. I am the auditor here to check the books. The casino is actually owned by a holding company and I have been sent by the accountancy firm to—"

"Shut up. I don't care about that. Where is he?"

"Greshenko?"

"Have I mentioned any other names since I arrived? Greshenko, Greshenko, G-R-E-S—"

"Greshenko, yes, I understand. You wish to know where he is. It is my understanding that he had business in Gaborone and left last night to drive down there." He glanced at his wristwatch.

"I expect he is in Francistown by now. I believe he said he would be gone for several days. Would you like me to take a message?"

Lenka's face had achieved his signature beet red color that meant someone was close to being fed to the crocodiles. "He is gone? What about the others? The men who work for him, where are they?"

"You mean the staff? I suppose they are at their posts. Shall I call them? The kitchen will be preparing luncheon by now, of course."

"No, you idiot. I mean the men who are his gang members."

"He has a gang? Oh, dear. Are you sure? That doesn't sound like Rra Greshenko. I think my superiors will not be happy to hear that. Ah…could you let me loose? I am having difficulty breathing, sir."

Lenka let the man go. He slumped back in his chair, and swallowed. Lenka drew his gun from its holster and pressed the business end of the barrel against the auditor's forehead. "Listen to me, imbecile, there are six men who arrived here three days ago. They wear black suits and ties and white shirts. They are his enforcers. I want you to tell me where they are or get me someone in here who can."

"Ummm…please don't pull that trigger. I have a family. I will tell you what you want to know."

"Good. Where are those men?"

"Ah, so sorry, but I think you might be mistaken about the men you mentioned."

"Just tell me where they are. What? Why am I mistaken?"

"Those men are missionaries and they are gone, too."

"They are…? You said, gone? What kind of missionaries? Do you think I am stupid? You are the stupid. Missionaries?"

"The suits and ties, sir. It is a uniform of a sort. They have come from America. They are called Jehovah's Witnesses. You know them. They work in pairs and knock on your door and give you a pamphlet. Here, they gave me one, see?"

He handed them a dog-eared copy of *The Watchtower*. Lenka slapped it out of his hand.

"You are a fool."

"No, really. I spoke to them just this morning. They were checking out of the hotel portion of this facility. They wouldn't be party to the gambling, of course and—"

"Checked out? Where do they go?"

"I believe they said the Okavango. It was part of their tour, they said. There was a mini-bus and—"

"No one is here? No Greshenko, no men in the suits?"

"I'm afraid not. Sorry."

Lenka spun on his heel and strode toward the door. "Come."

The men filed out and gathered around their vehicles.

"Now what?" It was times like this that Lenka needed Irena. She would know what to do next. The thought did not make him happy.

"Something about this doesn't smell right," Cszepanski said. "I think we need to get our asses back to the warehouse."

"I want those men and Greshenko. Call our people in Gaborone. Tell them to pick him up."

"I don't think he's there, Boss."

"He's not there? Then where is he?"

"He and those men are somewhere in the area. That man in the office has no idea where because he was paid to say those things and they aren't stupid enough to tell him where they really are."

"No? Why not?"

"Because they know you would beat it out of him if he did. He's nobody."

Lenka started for the door. "I'll kill him."

"Not here, not now. He isn't going anywhere but I'd bet my percentage in this operation that there are cops waiting for you to try. Then you're done. Think about it. Jehovah's Witnesses? Come on. We're being played again, Oleg. They're up to something and the only assets we have at the moment are back at the warehouse."

"But you left a guard."

"Yes, and I am beginning to think it wasn't enough."

Chapter Thirty-two

The moment Lenka's men left to join their boss at the casino, an SUV pulled up in front of the warehouse. The two men tasked to guard the building had clearly not anticipated any trouble so soon. They had their weapons slung barrel down over their shoulders. One, Alyosha, was facing away from the road to avoid the early sun which, because of his massive hangover, produced more pain than he was willing to endure. The second, Mitka, held a cigarette in one hand and sipped from a cup of coffee in the other. Caught in the moment, he hesitated before dropping either one or both of them when three men piled out of the car, covered the three meters that separated them, and put both men in a choke hold. They were disarmed, zip-tied, duct-taped, and dumped in the cargo area of the SUV. While two men disassembled their weapons and scattered the parts on the ground, a third spray-painted some words in Russian on the walls of the building. When he'd finished, he dropped a copy of *The Watchtower* on the doorstep, jumped into the car with the others, and sped away. The whole operation took no more than three and a half minutes.

Irena Davidova also awoke with a splitting headache and the sense that something bad was going to happen today. Dark premonitions were not a stranger to her. They had saved her life on one occasion and money on several others. Lenka was not in bed and didn't answer her call. So, most likely that would be the bad thing she feared. She closed her eyes and tried to think over the pounding in her head. Of course, he had gone gunning after Greshenko. The dunce just refused to accept the fact that Botswana was not Russia and the Kasane was not St. Petersburg and you just didn't run around killing people in the open. She showered and dressed, finished off the few aspirins left in the bottle and searched for a bottle with something containing alcohol. She found a half-full glass she'd left the night before. She drank it in one long pull, straightened her skirt, and stalked out the door.

Lenka had the auto, of course. That meant she needed a ride to the warehouse. She assumed he would be headed for the casino and hoped he would stop to pick up Cszepanski and men before he did. If she hurried, she might catch them before they left for the casino and botched what was left of the operation. If not, she'd be there to pick up the pieces, if there were any to pick up. The man at the front desk said he was sorry, but there were no taxis at the moment. Perhaps he could arrange a rental. It would take and hour or so but, he felt certain he could manage to find a car. She told him that she didn't have an hour. Outside, a man leaning on the driver's side door of the lodge's van listened to her story. He accepted a small bribe and agreed to drive her to the warehouse. He said he could not wait for her and she would have to find another way back. She said she understood and climbed in.

When Lenka and his crew returned to the warehouse, there were no guards inside or out. The walls of the building had been spray-painted in Russian, *Домой* had been applied in large red letters across the doorway and *Вашего народа, в прошлом* next to it and overlapped two panes of the adjacent window. They stepped out of the vehicles, guns drawn, eyes searching the surrounding shrubbery. There did not appear to be anyone around, including the two men left to keep watch.

"What has happened here?" Lenka's face began to redden. "Where are the men?"

"Gone." Cszepanski kicked open the warehouse door. He bent and picked up the magazine lying there and handed it to Lenka.

"What is this?"

"Is a copy of that missionary magazine the numbers man showed us back at the casino."

He tore it to shreds. "I think we go back there and shoot that man. I should have done it when I had the chance. He must be in on this."

"And I will guarantee that he is no longer there."

Cszepanski disappeared into the building. Lenka paced the parking lot, cocking and releasing the hammer on his gun, and muttering to himself. The other men gave him a wide berth. The two Boers shuffled out, glancing over their shoulders at a scowling Cszepanski. He herded them over to Lenka.

"These idiots were asleep, they say. They didn't hear or see anything."

"Something has happened?" asked the one they called Hans, confusion and fear in his eyes.

"Look for yourself, simpleton. You see what someone has done to the wall while you two idiots were sleeping?"

The two men pivoted and gazed at the spray-painted words. "Ja, sure we do. What's it say?"

It's Russian, you idiot. *Домой*, it means, 'Go home.' Someone dropped by and tells me I should go home. What do you think of that? Should I be going home? No? Okay. *Вашего народа, в прошлом*, is meaning 'Your people are gone.' There were two men posted here when we left. We call them the Karamazovs, you know why? It is because of their names, like the brothers. You know this book? No? You are idiots. So, two men with weapons. These men are very tough. The weapons are loaded. These men have killed for me. You understand? And now they are gone. Why are they gone? Who took them away? Of course you don't know. You are sleeping. Look on the ground. What do you see?"

The Boers scanned the ground around them. "Their weapons are in pieces scattered all over the place. Somebody field-stripped their automatic rifles."

"Ah, now you are getting smarter. So, some people drive up here, disarm two of my best men, take their weapons apart, spray-paint messages on the wall, and you hear nothing?"

"Nothing."

"Cszepanski, take these two around back and shoot them."

Whether the order would have been carried out they would never know. At that moment a van with markings that identified it as belonging to the Mowana Lodge pulled up and delivered Irena Davidova to them. The look in her eye and the set of her jaw meant that there would be words, shouting, and recriminations. When things went badly, there were always words, shouting, and recriminations. In the end, Irena would turn Lenka around and some sense of order would be returned to what they were attempting. But first, Lenka's earlier trip to the casino had to be unpacked and common sense restored.

The Boers, seeing their chance, slipped away. They would not return. By this time they had discerned that the man who paid them to bring trouble to the locals had slipped around the bend and their best chance to survive the next year or two meant heading back to Pretoria. As Cszepanski had noted, they were not the sharpest knives in the drawer, but they weren't Lenka's idiots either. Once it had been pointed out to them, they could read the handwriting on the wall. They found a quiet bottle store, bought drinks, and plotted their exit from Kasane. All they needed was money and transportation. Somehow they would manage that, they felt sure.

Modise stepped through the doorway after the office door closed behind Lenka and his people. He watched as they conferred and then drove away.

"You were amazing, Joseph. Such acting. I imagine you play a great Father Christmas. I will mention this in my report. That copy of the Jehovah's Witness paper was a masterful touch."

Joseph rubbed his forehead. "It was what you said for me to… Modise, he put that gun of his right here. He was very angry and I think a little crazy. I could have been killed."

"We had you covered the whole time."

"No, no you couldn't have. I mean it was right here between my eyes." Joseph put his forefinger on the still red spot between his eyebrows where Lenka had pressed his pistol. He exhaled and shook his head. "If he had pulled the trigger, I'm a dead man. You are in the other room ready to arrest him if he did it, yes, but there was no way you could have prevented it, Modise. I was the goat staked to the ground and bait for the jackal."

"Joseph…"

"Where's the loo? I think I'm going to be sick."

Modise pointed toward the hallway and Ikanya dashed through the door. Modise heard a second door bang open and then his colleague throwing up.

"You'll be fine, Joseph," he shouted. "It will be something to tell that baby of yours when he or she is older."

Joseph's only reply was a prolonged groan followed by more gagging. Modise couldn't blame him. He was right. Not even if they'd moved the instant Lenka leveled his gun at Joseph's head, could they have saved him if the Russian had pulled the trigger. Modise felt a little queasy himself and a little guilty as well.

Chapter Thirty-three

Dimitri Krasney and Alyosha Pitkin, the "Karamazovs," were surprised to learn three important things. First, the police and the army seemed to work together. Two, neither had a problem with civilians performing arrests even when the arrest included duct tape and spray-painting a building, and three, that carrying automatic weapons like the ones they had in their possession that morning fell into the category of a serious breach of the law. All of which explained why Cszepanski had told them earlier to be armed but also to stay indoors. As it happened, the tin roof on the warehouse turned it into an oven so they'd stepped outside to keep guard. Their crime was so serious, they were told, that they had to be temporarily incarcerated, not in the local jail, but in the barracks of the local unit of the Botswana Defense Force. They were dangerous men and the police feared they would influence the very few local miscreants currently in the general prison population. Not only that, but since none of them spoke Setswana, there was no one who could translate for them. Thus, the isolation. Their protests that everyone was speaking English and they did not need translators also ended up being ignored. They were Russian, yes? So, no translators available.

It came as a further shock to them when they discovered that two men who'd been arrested for poaching the day before were not only men they knew very well, but had shared the same fate. At least they now knew where and how their colleagues had disappeared. It began to dawn on one of the more perceptive of them that they were being used as pieces in a complicated game which had as its goal the destruction of Lenka. They demanded their phone call, their lawyer. Okay, not their lawyer, their barrister. Their captors merely shrugged and suggested they watched too much American television and that this was Botswana, not Boston. And things were done differently here. Their access to legal council had hit a small snag but, not to worry, in a few days they would be allowed to talk with a barrister. In the meantime, their visas had been revoked. In the unlikely event they were found not guilty of the crimes of which they were accused, they most certainly would be deported and they probably should worry about that more than when they would see legal counsel. There were outstanding warrants in two countries for three of the four.

The further protests from all four that they had been kidnapped and their arrests had been made by people who were Russian gangsters and not the police fell on deaf ears. The suggestion was absurd on its face, the captain told them. There were no gangsters in Botswana, Russian or otherwise, and if there were, how could the detainees possibly know about them?

They needed to understand that the Government of Botswana held very serious positions on poaching and the carrying weapons, any weapons. Very serious.

〉〉〉

The prisoners were nominally Superintendent Mwambe's to deal with. They had been rounded up in his area of responsibility. He did not know whether to be pleased or furious that Modise had recruited the BDF to handle them. Should he assume the responsibility and perhaps the credit for removing four dangerous felons from the general population, or should he report this travesty of justice to the director of the DIS and have Modise brought down a peg or two? For the moment, he decided to stay quiet and see how it all played out. If the operation that Modise had launched in his jurisdiction—without his knowledge, should be noted—failed, he would formally complain. If, on the other hand, it succeeded, he would take the plaudits.

What he couldn't understand was the change in his newest friend, Joseph Ikanya. When Ikanya had arrived from Gaborone to inspect and consult, they'd both agreed that the department needed a thorough review and a return to traditional policing. People like this Modise, for example, with his lack of regard for the experience of men older and wiser than he, needed to be disciplined. He, and men like him were much too young for command. At least that is how Mwambe remembered their conversations. Then, Inspector Ikanya volunteered to help Modise and now he had become a completely different person.

Ikanya had bounced into his office earlier gushing like a schoolboy. "Mwambe," he'd said, "I had forgotten what real police work was like."

Mwambe had puffed up a little at that and started to relate some of his more exciting stories about crime in Kasane, but was cut off. Ikanya blurted his adventures at the casino and how close he'd come to death. Mwambe had been appropriately shocked.

"You should report this malfeasance of office immediately. This Inspector Modise is acting without authority and endangering lives. Yes, Joseph, you should call the director."

"No, no, you miss my point. Yes, I was frightened and yes, I could have been killed, but don't you see, this is what we are called to do? This is police work, not sitting at a desk pushing paper about and making telephone calls to people who already know what you are about to tell them. It is about apprehending criminals and taking risks, not organizing motorcades and traffic details. If you are not willing to put your life on the line to insure that the law is kept, you do not belong in policing."

Mwambe didn't understand and changed the subject. Putting one's life on the line seemed excessive, particularly in light of the approach of his retirement. In fact, Mwambe had passed the correct age and had accrued the tenure necessary for retirement. He'd put it off mostly because he had settled into his position like one sinks in a soft sofa, an exceedingly comfortable sofa and at the same time, one difficult to get out of. So, he'd put off the business of filling out forms and all the fuss that went with that. He'd told Derek that if they wanted him to retire, they would say so. And besides, if he retired, what would become of his nephew? Mwambe had these thoughts swirling through his head as he, Ikanya, and Modise viewed the four prisoners through the one-way glass

Modise's voice cut through his musing. "Superintendent, are you able to accept this situation for a few days? I know it is irregular, but this whole situation is irregular. We have never had to confront criminals of this caliber before. They are organized and heavily armed. The BDF colonel tells me that these men had weapons more modern than those the government issued to his men. That can't be good. We broke their weapons down and left them on the ground as a message. Naturally, we removed and kept the firing pins. We couldn't leave that kind of dangerous material in working order. So, taking this Lenka down has to be job number one and done in such a way that no other group will attempt to repeat what he is up any time soon."

As he listened to Modise rattle on, Mwambe realized he was stuck between two equally unattractive choices. If he objected, Modise would overrule him and he'd look the fool if the operation succeeded. If it failed, he would be a hero, but he would be labeled as "not a team player." He thought that he might check into that retirement paperwork after all.

"We shall proceed as you suggest, Modise, but I have my reservations." There, he'd covered himself. He could play ball but his experience led him to suggest caution.

"Splendid. I will report to the director I have your full support." Modise excused himself and left the room before he could object. Ikanya beamed.

"This is exciting, don't you think? Oh, if you would like to be the person who fools the gangsters next time, I'll put in a word."

"Umm, ah, no thank you, Joseph, I am too close to retirement. Did you know? Yes, I believe that it may be my time to step down and let someone else take on the reins."

"Well, good for you, Mwambe. I hope you have a comfortable retirement. Shall I send for the forms, or perhaps you'd rather do that?"

"Modise, a moment." BDF Colonel Kande Ditau stopped Kgabo in the hall as he exited the room. "You realize we can only continue this charade for another day at the most?"

"I do. May I ask one more favor? When you turn these men over to Superintendent Mwambe, could you impress on him the need to keep them separate from the other prisoners and to find some pretext to hold off on the meeting with their barrister? I cannot know if this will crack open in time or not. We are doing things here that we have never done before."

"That seems pretty obvious to me. All day I have been receiving calls from Gaborone. They want to know about the poachers. I have to tell them we are building a case. They say, 'Well, are they poachers or not?' I am like a dancer here, Modise, tapping away. I cannot hold out much longer. So, tomorrow, Mwambe receives these men. I will impress on him the need to keep them incommunicado, but I cannot guarantee anything, you see. We are, after all, dealing with Mwambe." His mobile rang. He opened it and listened, nodded and snapped it shut. "Sorry, I must leave. There has been a road accident along A33 Road in Pandamatenga. A vehicle driven by a South African veered off the road and knocked down some of my men. One of them is dead and another in hospital. If that is not enough, now I hear there is another accident, a motorist died on the spot after an elephant attack. This is rapidly becoming a very bad day for me."

Modise thanked him. They both dashed out the door. The superintendent headed to Kasane Primary Hospital, Modise to his car. He'd told Sanderson he'd meet her at two and he was going to be late.

Chapter Thirty-four

Irena let Lenka pace and yell for fifteen minutes, then twenty. She sat in the corner chain-smoking one of Cszepanski's American cigarettes. Finally, Lenka paused in his ranting and searched the room. No one moved or spoke.

"Where are those two useless Boers? Why haven't you shot them? Why does everybody suddenly think they can ignore me, hey?"

Cszepanski waved a hand and studied his shoes. "It's not like that, Chief. Think a minute—"

"What? You think I don't think? I am thinking all the time. We are rich and powerful because I am always thinking. You are what? You are the one doing this thinking? You are not. You are working for me. I can have you eliminated anytime I wish, yes? Are you complaining about what we have, what you have? You can always go home to that place where you came from. Croatia isn't it?"

"Chief, that's not what this is all about and you know it. I am the loyal one, remember? How did you manage the Mirogoj Cemetery business except for what I knew about Zoltan Tsipsis? Okay? So listen. This is all I am saying. This Greshenko is not following the way we do things and still he is old Bratva. Why is that? He is Moscow Bratva, sure, but not so much difference, no? Something is all wrong here. You are told to vacate your room, but that is not the case. Somebody pretends to be the hotel management. Two men in suits that would usually mean they are security guard provided by Bratva, appear at hotel door. Then they are gone. Okay. Next, two and now two more of our people are snatched from us but, we don't know how. Also, they are in the wind. Nobody can find them. Not in the jail, not on the road south. Nowhere. Who can manage such a thing? And they say Greshenko is out of town. It makes no sense, is all I'm saying."

Lenka sat and accepted a chilled beer from Irena. It wasn't her time yet. She uncapped another for herself. No one else dared to risk being singled out and they sat as still as statues. They would get water, go to the bathroom later. Not now. Not with an angry Lenka in the room. Cszepanski needed to talk some sense into Oleg before Irena dared say anything.

"Except he could be dropping them in the river or the park like we do, no? Maybe he is just following the leader," Lenka said.

"Maybe, but I don't think so. Our Game Park gate operator would know and tell us."

"You trust him?"

"We have his daughter in a place. She only lives if he behaves. So, it's not a matter of trust. No, something is all wrong here."

"Okay, so what do you think is going on?"

"I don't know exactly, but I am guessing he is not the person calling the shots."

"Not Greshenko? Who then?"

"I don't know. Look, there were army trucks in play at one time. Is the army after us? How would that work? And who were the men in the suits, the so-called missionaries? They are a lot of things, I think, but being missionaries isn't one of them."

Irena judged that Lenka had calmed enough for her to risk inserting herself in the discussion. "The police," she said. "All the time it is the police. They are playing this game. We were right the first time. Greshenko is nothing. Greshenko is and always has been their stooge. They must have got to him before we did and they have set this up. So, while we think we are competing for territory and possessions with another Bratva gang, it is the police who are trying to destroy us. That is what they want, don't you see? They want us destroyed."

"You think?" Cszepanski hadn't quite thought of it that way but it made sense. More sense than any of Lenka's ideas anyway. Of course, that was nothing new, either.

"There is no other explanation for all this. Men do not disappear and we don't know where. A fake manager at hotel. What else?" Irena flicked a speck of lint from her skirt.

"So, if this were in St. Petersburg or any normal place, we would have a few important people in our pocket and the police would not be in play. But in this country, police are not available."

"Not yet," Lenka said.

"Not yet is right," Irena said. "And that is why we must change our plans. Forget Greshenko and his fake gang members. They are not important to us anymore. We need to break the police."

"How?"

"Ah. That is the question. Where is their weak point? What about that fat superintendent? What if we brought him here and demonstrated what happens to police if they do not cooperate and then show him some money to let him know what happens if they do."

Cszepanski shook his head and fumbled for the pack of cigarettes in his pocket. "I don't think so, Irena Davidova. His name is Mwambe and what I am hearing is, he is not involved. The word from the people who joined us after we removed Botlhokwa, he is nothing but a bag of wind. Anyway he is busy with some inspector from the capitol and…*Иисуса Христа*! I just remembered something. I knew I'd seen the little shrimp before."

"What little shrimp?"

"You weren't there, Irena. When we went to the casino this morning a man who said he was an auditor gave us a lot of crap about Greshenko. Anyway I saw him before but forgot. He's a policeman from Gaborone. He's been seen here and there with the fat one."

Lanka's fist hit the table. "I knew we should have shot him. Why did you stop me?"

"I just now remembered. Actually, it's a good thing you didn't. Now we know who and what he is, we can use him. We will tell him things that are false and lead them on the same roller coaster they put us on."

Irena swirled the beer in her glass and studied the floor. "Only if they are foolish enough to use him again. I don't think they will."

"No? Why not?"

"Because, Oleg, whether you are ready to admit it or not, they are not stupid. No, I think we must act more directly. The policeman we want is that man who meets with the woman game ranger. The one whose phone we cloned. Of course that didn't help much. He must have figured it out." Lenka started to object. "It doesn't matter if he did or didn't. Those two are close. Very close, I am betting. We snatch her and—"

Cszepanski cleared his throat and frowned. Disagreeing with either of these two included a measure of risk. "Too obvious. She is a very public person, always popping in and out of the police headquarters, driving around the town and the park. We need something subtler."

"Something or somebody?"

Cszepanski sat back and smiled. "Don't forget she has a daughter. I think that one is in university in Gaborone or thereabouts. Send someone to grab her. Put her with the other daughter. Then we take pictures. If that doesn't work, we strip her and take pictures. If that doesn't—"

"If that doesn't work, we start removing body parts." Lenka finished for her. "I like it. Make the call."

Irena shook her head. "Okay, we do that, but not just yet. We need to set the whole thing up. We need to put somebody on the policeman and the woman. We need to know where they meet and what they do. If we move too soon, they will split the operation"

"Split what?"

"They will pull this man off the effort to get us and bring in someone new. Then they will put a different group together just to find the kidnappers."

"But that will be us. So it is the same." Lenka sometimes had a hard time following Irena, especially when she talked fast.

"No, you miss the point. Yes, it is us in both cases and yes, they will overlap but, two units operating separately means twice as much to keep track of for us. Twice as many police poking around, you see? No we move slow."

"We do nothing?"

"Not nothing. We put car in neutral. Maybe low gear. Go slow. No matter what they do to try to goad us, we smile and just roll along, yes? That will make them angry."

"And?"

"And then two things. First we put eyes on the daughter and when they are busy with other things, we snatch her."

"Other things? What other things?"

"That is the second point. They will have to put Greshenko and his choir boys back in play and this time we will be the ones playing the game. Yes?"

"Yes."

Chapter Thirty-five

"Did I tell you I had a bad dream last night?"

"A bad dream? What could make Sanderson, who faces fierce wild beasts every day, have a bad dream?"

"You are poking at me, Kgabo. Anyway, it wasn't a dream, really. It was only that I woke up frightened and worried like you do when you have a bad dream, only I didn't. My *Nkuku* says that the crocodile is eating my *mowa*."

"What? Your Gran says crocodile ate your soul? What does that mean anyway?"

"It is a mystery. I think it is about a premonition that something bad is about to happen. Like that."

"And do you think that is so? Something bad will happen to you."

"Or to someone close to me, maybe. Yes. I worry about Mpitle and Michael since this business with the Russians began."

"But I told you I have them both under close surveillance. What is to worry about?"

"Mpitle says she sees no policeman anywhere. She thinks you are fooling just to make me feel better."

"That is the whole point of the surveillance. She should not see the cover. If someone is looking to do a bad thing with her, they will be caught because they don't see the person covering her."

"So there is someone around all the time?"

"She has a new roommate, yes?"

"Her roommate? Kopano Lekgwamolelo is a police constable?"

"She is that and more. She is also a student of criminal psychology at the university."

"And she can keep my daughter safe?"

"She has a black belt in karate and can shoot the eye out of a mosquito at twenty yards. Of course she can keep Mpitle safe."

"And Michael?"

"Covered."

"And me?"

"I am here."

"Ah, so that is how it is. Did you also know I can shoot the eye out of a mosquito?"

"At twenty yards?"

"Close enough. Twenty inches. But the end is the same, a blind mosquito."

◇◇◇

Irena and Lenka returned to their rooms at the lodge. A few buttons and some lovemaking that more nearly approximated calisthenics than romance and Lenka lay sprawled on the bed snoring. Irena studied her project. That had been the nature of their relation at first. He was her project. He needed to be refitted and re-imagined. Not that Lenka would have agreed. He had in mind that he'd moved her to heights of passion that she'd found irresistible. But for Irena, he was "the project." Now, the time approached when she would have to decide what to do with her project. Should she abandon it, reconstruct it, or play out the string and see where it all led? She sat and smoked and pondered. To do it now or later? Soon? She totted up the plusses and the minuses. Plus, she would leave now; minus, leave later. In either case, not if but when. A decision like that usually required a precipitating incident or event and so far, there had been none.

She stood and began her routine, checking his pockets, unloading his gun, securing money, and checking the notebook. She also opened his cellphone and read his e-mail, calendar, and deleted the pictures he'd taken of her earlier. He didn't see enough of her skin, he had to take pictures, too? For what, to show off to his friends? Idiot men. It is always about the conquest. She shook her head.

Danger Woman had only a few more days until she and her offspring would leave the lair and rejoin the pack. It would be larger now with the addition of her cubs and those of the other females. How long that growth would last would depend on her success as a leader and the ability to protect the very young and the very old. The latter were the least of her concern. When you could no longer hunt, your usefulness diminished and your place in the pack became tenuous. Unlike Irena Davidova, Kotsi Mosadi did not have the gift of logic, the ability to assign a weight to potential decisions. A graceful retirement to a comfortable *dacha* in the suburbs surrounded by friends and family would not be her future. When the time came, it would be because she had lost a step, had been careless, or had been caught completely unaware. Then she would fall to the crushing jaws of a big cat, a lion more than likely, or the slashing jaws of one of her own.

She began her routine. She tested the air, listened, and stared into the bush. She started one way and stopped. Nothing moved. She started in another direction and stopped again. Nothing. Assured, she trotted off to seek nourishment.

All of this was duly noted by Ole Andersen. His brows furrowed briefly. Something was not right. Alone, Danger Woman usually took more time to assess her surroundings. In the past, she would make at least four, sometimes a dozen feints to one path or another. She would be absolutely sure of her safety before starting off. He swung the camera on its pivot and tracked her into the bush. Since he felt sure the river was not her destination, he had no idea where she might be headed. He would wait for her return. But something didn't feel right about this day.

He wondered how much of his anxiety stemmed from his concern about Kotsi Mosadi and how much from his daughter's news. Michael Sanderson was a good boy, but where could this end? How could it possibly work? He wanted his daughter to be happy, yes. He also wanted her to marry and have babies. He harbored a picture in his mind of grandchildren, many grandchildren. But, that would never happen if Sekgele married this man. Did Michael's mother know? Was it his place to say anything? Raising a daughter alone had been difficult enough. Now this. His wife would have known what to do. He missed her more now than when she'd first passed away, strange as that might seem. He supposed it had to do with seeing how much his daughter had grown to resemble her mother. He sighed. What to do?

◇◇◇

Mpitle saw the man standing at the corner. "Kopano, do you see that man over at the corner?"

"Yes, so what?"

"I think he must be the constable my mother says is watching me. He is there all the time and he is looking at me every time I come out of the building."

"And you see him all the time?"

Yes, well, I think so."

"And you find this suspicious? You are very pretty. I should think men will stare at you a lot. So, what is different here?"

"For one thing, he is pretending to read that newspaper but he never turns the pages. How long does it take to read a page? Then he is an older white man, defiantly not Motswana, who is reading *Mmegi?* And then why always on that corner?"

"Really, I think you have taken up the wrong major field of study, Mpitle. You are very observant. You should be studying art, not engineering."

"I would like to but, my mother would kill me if I did. She says I can't make a place in the world drawing pictures."

"Well, we must listen to our mothers, but I think she is mistaken. Excuse me but, I have to make a call. You keep walking. I don't want you to be late for your classes. I will catch up with you in a minute."

She turned aside and made a series of calls

Fifteen minutes later a van pulled up to the corner and another member of Lenka's group of thieves and criminals disappeared without a trace.

This news made its way to the warehouse and to Cszepanski. He thought about what it meant, what Lenka would do if he knew, and decided the best course would be to not mention it until after he had a chance to talk in greater detail with the people in Gaborone. After all, Nicolai Zoran had never demonstrated any measure of brilliance and his disappearance might just as easily be due to his stupidity as police acuity. He ordered another man put on "Daughter Watch" and specified that this time it be someone with subtlety. He had to explain what he meant by "subtlety." He rolled back in the swivel chair behind his desk and watched as the Boers played some card game which seemed to consist of slapping the cards down hard on the table while barking "Ha!" and then laughing uproariously. Something had to be done about these morons.

His thoughts turned back to the missing Nikolai. That made five men who'd disappeared into thin air. He wondered at that. Obviously this had nothing to do with Greshenko, at least not directly. It supported Davidova's notion that it must be the government calling the shots, not Greshenko. Someone observing him had once noted that Cszepanski's greatest strength resided in that part of his brain which monitored his self awareness. Cszepanski knew his limitations. That same person once told him that a wise man wasn't measured by what he knew but by what he knew he didn't know. In that equation Lenka did not qualify as wise. Davidova...Cszepanski wasn't sure whether she knew her weaknesses or not, or cared. But he knew when a noose began to tightened on his neck and when it did, he'd need to work up some alternatives. He thought the noose had begun to squeeze a bit lately.

In truth, he felt completely lost in this strange nation which valued the future of its wild animals nearly as much as it did its people. A country which shipped in rhinos at huge expense, and then committed its army to prevent poaching of those animals and all the other denizens of their game parks. A country that seemed incorruptible. He found that phenomenon the most puzzling. How could a person like Lenka or him possibly make their way in a place like that?

He pocketed the keys to one of the trucks, told one of the Boers to gas it up. He wanted to have a guaranteed exit from the Chobe if, and when, the need arose. He was beginning to sense that there was no *if.*

Chapter Thirty-six

Yuri Greshenko had placed himself on a strict regimen of coffee, gallons of it. No more booze until this whole business with Lenka ended. Alcohol makes you careless and slows you down. The old black-and-white American movies where the hero downed tumblers full of whiskey and then proceeded to take on the bad men with no apparent side effects made him laugh. In his experience the best way to deal with someone who planned to hurt you was to buy them a few drinks. Sooner or later, they would take themselves out of play. Yuri had spent his youth in an environment where strong drink and lots of it constituted the norm. Russia had more alcoholics than people, he used to say. Most of those who heard him say it back in the old country did not see the joke. "How can that be?" they'd ask and pour themselves another vodka. A nation of drunks. At any rate, if anyone had a tolerance for ethanol in its various forms and flavors, it would be Yuri, and he knew he couldn't run the risk of losing even a nanosecond in his own reaction time. So, for now, no booze.

On the other hand a few stiff drinks might ease the sense of foreboding that had followed him around all day. His years in the life gave him a second sense about these things. He knew in his bones that all hell was about to break loose and soon. He did not know the where or the when of it, only that it would. Moreover, he did not believe Inspector Modise had a clue as to the seriousness of the situation. True, it had not been the policeman's plan to taunt Lenka in the first place, so Modise should be given a break. The little cop had only wanted to spy on Lenka, find the weak spot in his organization, and then deport him and the rest of his crew back to Russia, including that woman. It had been Leo Painter who had ratcheted the operation up ten notches. Deportation seemed like a pretty good idea at the time, but since Leo feared that Yuri's life would be the price to be paid for any move against Lenka, he'd upped the stakes. His assumption had been that doing so gave Yuri a better chance to survive. For that Yuri owed Leo, but now it was beginning to look like a lot of people were going to have to die, himself included. So, not quite the trade-off Leo had in mind. One thing he knew for sure, somebody was going to die. The goal now had become…what? Yuri wasn't sure about the end game. He wasn't sure anyone else was either. Yuri knew that bad things were on their way as clearly as he knew that come Sunday he should be in a church somewhere praying for forgiveness for all his sins. But first, he needed to survive the next few days. Then, maybe after all this ended, he'd chance it. Were there any Orthodox churches in Botswana? He'd have to look that up. Did it matter?

When he thought about it, he realized that the real problem rose from the failure on both sides to acknowledge the shape and capabilities of the other. For his part, Lenka believed the police and the indigent culture were stupid, backwards, and incapable of responding to threats in any real way. This bigotry Lenka shared with all of his crew and it would be their undoing. At the same time, the local police understanding of gangs stemmed from a simplistic model based on studies of urban America. Modise and his compatriots had failed to grasp the predictable behavior which would be the expected outcome of the implacable brutality and willingness of the Bratva to shed blood, terrorize, and torture. You would have thought, he mused, that living so close to the wild as the Batswana did, where it is be predator or be prey, where life is lived out in the moment, and where mercy is not even a concept, that they would, by now, have come to understand that the Bratva were more like those animals than movie gangsters. They were predators, not the cast from *West Side Story.*

In any case, the game had changed. By now, Lenka or his brains—he guessed that would be the woman, Davidova—should have figured out that their competitor was not him and the six business associates of Leo Painter posing as Ukrainian thugs, but the police. Once they got that straight, if they hadn't already, really bad things were going to happen and win or lose, the Chobe would never be the same again. He decided to call Modise. It was time to rethink this operation and the six naïve and eager guys from Chicago headed the list of things needing rethinking. They had had some fun, some very risky fun. It was time to send them home. He picked up the phone and made the call.

Nothing short of a miracle could stop what was shaping up to be an epic train wreck.

A telephone call was not something Modise wanted at that exact moment. Any interruption would not have been welcome. He decided to push the NOT ACCEPT option.

"Who was that?" Sanderson asked.

Kgabo glanced at the phone, and tapped RECENT. "Greshenko."

"Shouldn't you answer it? It could be important."

Modise rolled over with a groan. How did that old time musical show say it? Rra Gilbert? Yes, "A policeman's lot is not a happy one." He hit RE-DIAL and waited.

"So sorry, Rra Greshenko, I had my hands full when you called." Sanderson failed to suppress a yelp. "Who? No, it is the…dog. There is a dog outside that is making barking sounds. Yes." Sanderson buried her face in the pillow. "What do I think Lenka will do next? He will attack you from a different direction. But you do not need to worry, we are covered."

Modise listened. His eyebrows shot up and he held the phone away from his ear. He looked at Sanderson and put one finger to his lips. She grinned and listened. Greshenko did not sound happy.

"Yes, I know they have shifted their strategy a bit. They tried to kidnap Mma Michael's daughter in Gabz. So, yes, I agree they have determined that you alone are not the person who torments them. I insist, however that the man, Lenka, is also a narrow thinker and…What? Narrow? He is not too broad in his thinking. He is limited in the brains department and has not forgiven you for hurting his man Grelnikov. He might…no, make that, she. That Davidova woman will think to come after us, the police, but will still go after you and your friends. They will argue and make mistakes because their efforts are divided. One very big mistake and away they will go."

Modise listened for another few minutes.

"No, I don't think those fake gangsters you are housing should return home. Rra Painter brought them here and put them in the game, you could say. So, they are now part of the show. If they disappear, the balance is removed from the board. What? I am speaking in term of a game, that sort of board. Greshenko, whether it was Rra Painter's plan or not, those men are now committed. They are the bait. If we wish to hunt big game, it is always easier if you set out bait. A goat or a heifer tethered to a stake. I am sorry for those men. I am sure they thought this would be a great and exciting adventure, something to regale their children and grandchildren with, but this is serious business. I cannot make them stay in Kasane, but I can keep them in the country. Whether they are tethered to a stake here or someplace else, in Gaborone or in Kasane, it makes no difference. They are bait."

Kabo turned to Sanderson. "He hung up. Can you imagine? He is not happy with the police. So, now where were we?"

"You were doing something naughty with your thumb."

Chapter Thirty-seven

This would be the last time Kotsi Mosadi would hunt alone, at least for a year, until the next reproductive cycle came around. She checked back to make sure her offspring were secure in the lair. She tested the wind. It blew from the south. If there were lions in their lolling spot she'd know it. The air held many scents but no lions today. She trotted off in the same direction she'd used for the past two days. There would be game on the far side of a large cleared area. She had only to transverse it and she would be relatively safe and in a position to hunt, feed, and return to her burrow. She paused and sniffed again. Something? She hesitated, then, a decision made, padded out in the open and angled her path to make the crossing as short as possible.

Ole Anderson worried about Danger Woman's decision to follow the same track. Twice would be unusual, but three times in a row? If the hyena were her usual self, he should not be in any position to record her. He might guess her next move but it would be just that—a guess, yet here he was and there went Danger Woman on her way to hunt. He spun around as if he were Danger Woman's second in command and charged with securing the area. He saw nothing.

Of course he didn't. In the bush, people die because they don't see the thing right under their nose.

Animals, too.

Sanderson sat up, wide awake and shaking. "Something has happened," she cried. "Kgabo, what has happened?"

"What? Something has happened? When? Where? Sanderson, nothing has happened."

Both of their phones lit up at the same time.

"What has happened?" they both asked, then listened.

"No!" Again, simultaneously, then, "Thank you." They hung up and turned to each other.

"I have to go. You too? What did you hear? Never mind, I have to go. I'll tell you later. But, *no mathata.*"

He was lying.

She was sorry.

It took nearly a half hour for Sanderson to dress, find a suitable vehicle, and head out into the park. There were two SUVs on the lot. One, the doorless model caught her attention. She made yet another mental note to call Michael and ask him what was holding up replacing the doors on the machine. As it stood, it was useless. She climbed into the other and headed for the park.

She had only a rough idea where the Hyena Man had set up his observation. She found him slumped in the seat of his SUV. He looked terrible.

"She's over there." He said and pointed in the direction of some brush.

Sanderson squinted against the late afternoon sun and could just make out evidence of a struggle and the broken body of Kotsi Mosadi. "So, Rra Andersen, how does this happen?"

He waved a limp hand at the camera. "Push playback."

Sanderson crouched so she could see the small screen and pressed the button. She watched as a miniature Kotsi Mosadi trotted across the clearing, paused, pivoted, and then made a frantic dash for the bush. At the same moment, what appeared as a blur of tawny yellow streaked from the north and across the veldt straight at her. The hyena zigged and zagged but it could not evade the lioness which overtook her and pounced. The two animals rolled in a cloud of dust and settled in a heap, the lion on top. Sanderson shook her head and tsked as she watched the lioness clamp its jaws around Kotsi Mosadi's neck. A minute passed, two…Kotsi Mosadi went limp. The lioness shook her prey quickly and violently enough to tear out its throat. As if it needed to make absolutely sure its victim was dead. It rose up on all four feet and opened its jaws. Kotsi Mosadi crumpled to the ground. The lioness stared at it in what Sanderson would later describe as disgust, and loped away.

Two ancient enemies had clashed and one of them had died.

Ole, she saw, was disconsolate. For him the hyena was like family. She patted him on the shoulder. "It is the way, Rra Sekgele. We live in this wild place and we know it has rules. Nothing dies of old age in the wild. Danger Woman is for the *manong* now and soon a new and younger pack leader emerges. Too bad for Kotsi Mosadi, but probably good for the pack, yes?"

What else could she say? She felt relieved that the foreboding that had haunted her these last few days had been about the hyena, not something closer. She breathed a sigh of relief.

The television blared in the corner as a reporter nattered on about the shootout near the university.

"A man attempting to kidnap a student fired at the police earlier this afternoon. The police at the scene returned fire and the reports say the alleged kidnapper has been killed. Also, a constable might have been wounded. The identities of the alleged kidnapper and the wounded police officer have not been released nor has the reason the police on the scene arrived so quickly and already armed. The details of the attempted kidnapping were being withheld by the police pending further investigation. Early reports suggested the shooter might be a man who had been seen loitering about the premises for days. In other news, police are investigating a possible case of money laundering involving a thirty-nine-year-old man of Moroka and a woman of Gaborone. The man—"

Modise covered the mouthpiece of the telephone in his hand and snapped, "Shut that thing off." This was not good. So, someone had made another attempt to grab Mpitle and it appeared Constable Lekgwamolelo had been shot. How was Sanderson going to react to this? How would he tell her? She had a feeling something bad would happen and now it had.

"It is too bad," the director was saying on the phone, "that this man is shot dead. It would have been helpful if we could have made an identification and linked him directly to Lenka. As it now stands, your operation is no closer to being concluded and a man is dead, a constable wounded. Modise, wind this up. Wind it up now. That is an order." The director hung up.

Modise heard the threat in the director's tone but that did not concern him just yet. He'd put his career on the line when he'd listened to Leo Painter in the first place and everything else, good or bad, followed from that decision. There would be no turning back now. He'd wind it up, alright, but, maybe not the way the director wanted. So, he had provided protection and it had worked out exactly as it should have. The country now had one less gangster to worry about and the people who labored under the silly notion that Botswana was a nation of animal preservation freaks, unable to protect itself, now knew better. More importantly, in spite of what the director believed, that man would never have talked if he'd been taken alive. He was Bratva. Their motto, "I will yield to no man," as silly as it sounds to civilians, is a part of their nature and as permanent as the tattoos they acquire which mark their journey into the world of crime. No, what worried Modise at this moment was, what will Lenka would do next? His hand had been tipped a little... no, a great deal. He wanted to get at the police, at him, through Sanderson. That being the case, where would he turn up next?

"Phone for you, Inspector." A young man handed him a land line, eyes bright with the excitement a first real shooting incident will produce in a rookie policeman.

Greshenko. "You'd better get your ass over here in a New York...I forget what, minute, second? Now, Modise. I am looking at my parking lot. I have men in SUVs and they do not look friendly. My fake Ukrainian Cossacks are loading their guns and I halfway think at any minute they will break out into a damned marching song like the freaking Hitler Youth or something. They still think this is a picnic with fireworks. Modise, this cannot not end well. Hey, what did I say to you before? People are going to die today. You should listen better, Mister Policeman."

"One is dead already, one of theirs, in fact. If they know about it, and I guess they must by now, you are correct. Something bad is going to happen. Don't shoot unless you absolutely have to. Look for a BDF truck."

Modise hung up, grabbed four constables, had rifles issued to them. All but one of them held the rifle as if it were a snake. Guns of any sort were foreign to most of them. They had received training in their usage, fired them on the range but, to actually turn them on another human being? Modise ignored them. So, they had scruples. An admirable trait, but there was no time for lectures on police responsibility in dangerous situations. He loaded them into the borrowed BDF truck.

"No shooting unless I say to," he said and slipped behind the wheel.

"*No mathata*," One of them replied. If Modise hadn't been so wrapped up in what he had to do next, he might have wondered at the tone of the reply. Did she sound relieved or eager?

With any luck, he thought, the arrival of the BDF should send Lenka and his boys back to their den to rethink. He hoped so, anyway. The truck with its reluctant warriors roared out of the police lot and headed toward the river and its hotels.

Chapter Thirty-eight

Modise spun the truck into the casino parking lot scattering gravel in a wide arc. He roared past the line of black SUVs which were parked in a semicircle facing the front entrance. He reversed and backed to the main door. He didn't want the people in Lenka's cars to see that there were no soldiers, only police constables, in the back.

"Get out," he said. "Don't let them see you. Go straight inside and find cover and under no circumstances do you shoot unless I say so. If the shooting does start, I want you to aim at the autos, not the people. Shoot out headlights, tires, and things like that. Only if it is to save a life…yours in particular…should you aim at a person. Understood?"

The constables jumped from the back of the truck and scuttled into the casino. Modise called Greshenko.

"Tell your fake Cossacks to hold their fire. If the shooting begins, they are to try to shoot at the vehicles only. We don't kill people in this country except if they want us to. What do I mean? If they are foolish enough to shoot at us, we reply. Otherwise, we wait for them to see the sense in complying to a request to submit to arrest. So, that is how it is meant. I do not care if the Russians do not play the game that way. No, you are wrong. It is only counterintuitive in your world. Here it is the norm. We are not in Russia or the United States, either, and the sooner they and you come to understand that simple fact, by the way, the sooner we can settle this."

Modise retrieved a megaphone from under the seat and leaned out of the window. "Whoever you are. This is Police Inspector Kgabo Modise speaking. You are to disperse immediately. You are disturbing the peace and causing a public nuisance. Please leave now." He couldn't be sure, but he thought he heard laughter from both the vehicles arrayed against him and from within the casino. "I do not wish to repeat this. You are in violation of the legal code and you are to disperse. If you fail to do so, the BDF will move out and my officers will be required to arrest you. You have ten seconds…You have five seconds…You have—"

The cars moved slowly at first and then more quickly and drove off in different directions. That fact worried Modise. They should have all gone together to the warehouse that served as Lenka's headquarters. What were they up to now?

Greshenko appeared by the driver side door. "Somehow, Modise, you have pulled this off. I would not have believed it if I hadn't seen it with my own two eyes. What is it about this country that makes everybody act completely ass backwards?"

"Possibly it is because we are below the Equator which makes us upside down to Russia? No? It is because this is who we are and even though we know Lenka is not so smart, we know that he is not stupid enough to start a fire fight with either the army or the police. He will intimidate and he will even assassinate but these things he does in the dark where no one can see him. Out in the open? No, not happening."

"Then you think we are done here tonight?"

"I would like to think so but, no. Keep yourselves alert. They might return in the dark and unseen. You saw they split up. They have other things they are doing tonight. One of your men or all of them may be on their list. I am thinking that this is only a ploy to draw us here so they can do something elsewhere."

"Something else?"

"They have already made two attempts to kidnap Ranger Sanderson's daughter. One of theirs is dead. One of ours wounded. I don't know how badly. I don't think they will try for any of her people again anytime soon. You are another story.

They might come after you, but I don't think so. No, they will be in town this night and after other officials, what they see as weak spots in the system. Whatever they do, they must do it in a way that cannot be laid at their doorstep later. I think I will be looking for men wearing ski masks this night."

"I'll tell 'the Cossacks' to stay alert. Good night, Kgabo."

Modise called in and told Dispatch to put all police and staff persons on high alert. If they could move their families to relatives, they were to do so. He also suggested they extinguish their lights.

◇◇◇

A town which has no street lighting may be thought as an encourager of crime. In most places it is. But in the Chobe, darkness with its ever-present wildlife, separated from civilization and people by not much more than habit, can be a deterrent. At least it is if you are from Russia and can't tell a monkey from an elephant in the dark. Darkness can be good and it can be bad. It all depends on what you intend to do in it.

Almost no one knew Superintendent Mwambe's full name. People simply referred to him as Superintendent. Even Derek, his thick nephew, would be hard-pressed to come up with a name. His late wife called him Bubby, a name which had nothing whatsoever to do with his given name. Lenka said he didn't, for the Great God's sake, care what his name was. He wanted two men to visit him and suggest that the fat policeman fall into line. That is, if he didn't want an accident to happen to him or his family, he should consider taking a less aggressive stand when called on to persecute Lenka's men. It was a simple request, no? If he wasn't stupid, he would yield. Police, in Lenka's experience understood the use of power and the compromises it entailed. As far as family went, Lenka did not know that Mwambe's family consisted only of Derek Kgasa and threats in that direction would not produce much in the way of a reaction. Nevertheless, two men, sweating in woolen ski masks, set out for the police superintendent's house to deliver Lenka's message. They paused at the door, flexed their shoulders, and knocked.

Mwambe had received the alert. He'd snorted at Modise and his theatrics and had returned to his television program. He answered the knock at his door. He always did. It was that kind of neighborhood. When he saw the ski masks he realized he should have paid more attention to Modise's warning.

"What do you two men want?"

One of them produced a pistol from his waistband. "Move it," he said.

"You are breaking the law and I will be forced to arrest you."

"How's that again, Fat Man?"

"You have a firearm and I am certain you have no permit. I must ask you to surrender the pistol and both of you, please place yourselves on the ground."

"You do not understand, Fatso, we're coming in and you're going to listen. He shoved hard at Mwambe expecting him to crash into the furniture and then to the floor.

For a large man, Mwambe was very agile and like many others like him, light on his feet. He could dance. Even young women would choose him for a partner because of his dancing skills. He had exceptional balance and one might even say grace. People who did not like him called Mwambe the Dancing Hippo, but they had to concede that he did have the moves. At any rate, a push from even a well-muscled thug would not cause him to stagger, much less fall down. Instead of tumbling to the ground as the masked man assumed he would, Mwambe pivoted anticlockwise, a smooth pirouette, left arm extended, right tucked close to his chest. As his assailant came even with him, his closed left fist clipped the back of the man's neck. He, in turn, sailed across the small room and landed headfirst against the wall. His gun skittered along the floor and came to rest in a corner.

Mwambe continued his spin and as he approached its final, three hundred and sixtieth degree, he unleashed his right arm and planted his fist into the second man's face. Mwambe's fist, like the rest of him, was unusually large. Bone and cartilage cracked and the second man howled. Before he could raise his pistol, Mwambe knocked it from his hand. He grabbed the man's shirt front, yanked and then stuck out a leg and tripped him. He landed facedown next to the first who, as yet, showed no signs of movement, probably because his head had made a substantial dent in Mwambe's living room wall. The two ski-masked thugs lay side by side on the floor. Mwambe put handcuffs on the one with the broken nose and searched for and found a zip-tie for the other. Then he called headquarters and asked for a squad to come and collect two bad men he'd arrested. They should hurry, he said, because he was missing some very good telly.

Two more of Lenka's feared gangsters disappeared that night.

Mwambe might be inefficient, out of date, and socially irrelevant. He might not have seemed even important enough for people to bother to learn his name, but no one ever accused Mwambe of cowardice.

Chapter Thirty-nine

Grelnikov's attempts to doctor his own wounds failed and he'd collapsed in a restaurant across the street from his hotel. From there, an ambulance had taken him to a clinic. His doctors insisted he needed more bed rest. His broken ribs had not completely healed. The bones had not adequately knit. Any stress and they could separate again and he would be in real trouble. His vital signs, while greatly improved, were still those of a man in recovery. He needed complete bed rest for a week and then only light work.

While Lenka's men had been busy stumbling around in the dark, Grelnikov got out of bed and dressed. He muttered something in Russian that could have been, probably was, a racial slur, threw a handful of Zim dollars on the table and self-discharged. He hired a cab to take him from Hwange to Victoria Falls. He crossed into Zambia with an eye to proceeding from there into Botswana at the Chobe crossing and then catching a ride to Kasane. He had unfinished business in that town. After that, he would rest in bed.

All of the nurses and other staff members, while having concerns about him from a medical point of view, were relieved at his decision. He had been a difficult patient, for sure.

〉〉〉

Whether in southern Africa or the far northern reaches of Finland, morning sunlight tends to wash everything clean and prepare one for a new day, a new beginning. If the night has been daunting, mornings are hopeful, optimistic. They bring the promise of better things, better times, and who knows what else?

Superintendent Mwambe licked his finger and dabbed up the last crumbs of his morning muffin from his plate. "You know, Joseph, you may have a point."

For the previous five minutes Inspector Ikanya had been fascinated, watching Mwambe's search and destroy mission with his buttered muffin. "Point? What sort of point are we discussing, Motsu?"

"This retirement business. I had a terrible realization last night. I came to an epiphany, you could say. Epiphany…is that the correct word? I discovered something I should have been seeing all along, anyway."

"And what was that?"

"I am a dinosaur, Joseph. No, it is true. The world has changed and I have not kept up. It is that simple. I do not like women in positions I believe should be held by men. There, I said it. It is what I believe. I am not alone in thinking this, but there are fewer of us who feel that way every day. I know that. I am of that generation that looked to older and wiser leadership which the *Kgosi* provided. They were men of great stature and wisdom, the Four Kings. Now we have this *Kgosi Mosadi*. Is she wise? I don't know. We had the *kgotla* for ordinary justice. Now? Now it is mostly for meetings and talking. Policing meant picking up petty thieves and men who didn't understand what alcohol would do to their persons. Some motor mishaps on the roads and bad behavior. Now, it is crime of great proportions. Russian gangsters, smugglers, poachers, and thieves who will murder for a ten pula note. It has changed. I do not fit in anymore."

"What are you saying?"

"Ah, Joseph, I was a small boy when the great *Kgosi*, Sir Seretse Khama, returned to Botswana from England with his Ruth and we were set free from British rule. Those were great days. We built a nation then, Joseph. Amazing and challenging times, they were. Now, we are just one of many nations finding our way in the world. Civilization, which we all wished for, is here and as the saying goes, 'be careful what you wish for, you may get it,' yes? It is time for new people to be in charge. Last night I had to disarm two men who came to kill me or perhaps not. I never asked why they had guns aimed at me, but they did. I think they were up to no good and had murder in their hearts. It is not what we are used to, Joseph, this evil gangster business. It was at that moment I realized that in this stage of our country's development, the police must be the Modises, not the Mwambes. We must step aside and turn this new creation over to them."

"Mwambe, surely…"

"I will be forwarding my retirement papers to the director as soon as the business with the Russian gangsters is done."

Modise burst through the door. "Superintendent Mwambe, I heard. Are you quite alright?"

"I am fine, Inspector Modise. Those men are the sort who will underestimate a man if they find him amusing or not enough like them. If they had done their homework, they would have known not to get within a meter of me. But, all they saw was an old, out of date, fat policeman and assumed they would have an easy time of it."

"Well, you certainly did yourself proud. The men are in the lockup with their friends. Sooner or later, Lenka will run out of criminals to put in the field and will have to do his dirty work himself. Then we will have him."

"I would hope," Mwambe said, "that you will have him before he does any dirty business. It is time to restore the Chobe to its natural state. As long as you and these criminals are crashing about, there can be no peace. Where will the tourists go now? How shall we exist when we can't know from one minute to the next if shooting will start, if *bakkies* and *combies* filled with dangerous men aren't racing down our streets frightening everything, including the animals? Modise, you must end this and end it now."

"At least you and the director agree on that. You are correct it must end, but please understand that we are not like the police in the cinema. We do not go out with guns blazing. You know better than anyone, that we are not armed. If this is to end, it will be when Lenka takes a wrong step. He has come close. We are interrogating our prisoners, yours especially. You also should know that they will not give their boss up. The Bratva is a cruel and brutal organization whose reach can even find its way into our prisons. The men you took out believe that if they talk, if they implicate their leader, they will die. Not just die, suffer and then die. It is, as they say, the tough nut to crack."

"We understand that," Joseph Ikanya said, "but you have those American men. They seem more than eager to do something. Why not turn them loose on Lenka and when they're done shooting up each other, you step in and jail the lot of them?"

"The Americans, too?"

"Why not? There is a very good reason all this started and it is because that rich American who has left built a casino. It is too big a plum to have not attracted some attention from criminals. Of course they would come and they will keep coming as long as it sits there on the river. It is a criminal magnet. So, the Americans who began all this, the ones who survive the face-off, yes, jail them as well."

"Well, that is one way to look at it. I believe, however, that the builder of this casino had the government's blessing. That's one. Two, he has turned it into a Botswana-based corporation and has put an expat Russian in charge. Also it is not the first or only casino in the country. Anyway, blame-placing is not a productive use of our time just now. We need a quick and decisive move by one side or the other to finish this. Until that occurs, we wait."

Mwambe stood, pulled his shoulders back. "Inspector Modise, what can I do to help?"

"You have done quite enough already, Superintendent."

"I feel I am not done. Can you suggest something? Perhaps more misinformation on that funny phone?"

"Not that. By now they have tumbled to the fact we have been deceiving them. No, I think something closer to home.

Superintendent, what do you believe those men were up to when they visited you last night?"

"I rather imagine they wished to intimidate me. It occurred to me they had in mind to turn me into their inside man. Do you suppose they might still?"

"No, I think they will have let that thought go. However, do you think you might want to return the kindness? I am wondering if that warehouse they use as a headquarters can pass a fire inspection? I wonder if a search of the premises might produce contraband. Do you suppose a search warrant might be available to make a sweep like that? As the local Superintendent of Police, doubtless, it should be led by you."

"Ah, their lair. An excellent suggestion. Ikanya was about to say the same thing. Yes, four or five of us might be needed to accomplish that. We will need to recruit some help."

"Perhaps Greshenko's Americans would make themselves available. You could deputize them."

"Is that the correct word, deputize? It is not a thing I am familiar with. Do we do that? It sounds very American Wild West, don't you think?"

"I am afraid this whole operation has become like the American Wild West."

"Indeed, and certainly not my sort of thing. Very good, I will see to the warrant and, ah…deputize the cowboys. We will have a group to gallop off…what do they call them?"

"A posse?"

"Exactly, a posse. We will have a posse. Meanwhile, you could have a chat with Rra Greshenko about loaning us his friends."

Chapter Forty

For the last hour Lenka had been pacing and screaming at the people who still counted themselves as part of his group. Not only had the two he'd sent to Mwambe's house disappeared, but three more were seen taking a Botswana Air flight to Gaborone and presumably back to where they'd come from. His face acquired a shade of red new even for him. Emotionally, he stood on the cusp, the downward side of which led to near insanity. Irena recognized the symptoms and thanked Saint Nickolai, the patron saint of whores, that she'd had the foresight to unload his gun. Otherwise she would have been in a panic. If Oleg lost it, slipped over the line, he'd have to load and cock his weapon. That should give her enough time to escape or draw the nickel-plated pistol she kept in her purse and shoot him first.

Lenka pulled up short in front of her. "Somebody please tell me how a stupid fat black cop can put two trained men in jail. Is he a fat Superman, maybe? Under his uniform is big S? He is a wizard? What do they call them here, *moloi*? Cszepanski, tell me how this happens."

Irena lit a cigarette and released the snap on her purse. Her hand dropped in and felt the oily smoothness of the .038 automatic nestled in with her facial tissues, lipstick, pillbox, and passport. "It happens," she cut in, "when you underestimate your enemy. We have had this conversation before and still we ask the same questions. 'How do they do it?' and then make the same answers. Are we so stupid? They are not super men or super anythings. They are just making moves we don't expect them to make. We are used to police who can be persuaded to look the other way. We keep forgetting that here they don't look away. Is complex game, Oleg, and they are making the rules. Look, first these Ukrainians show up and we think they are Bratva and belonging to Greshenko. Next thing, they are gone to Okavango. Now they are with police ransacking our goods and speaking English like Americans. You see?"

"What's to see? Greshenko, do you think he is the one who has bought police, maybe? How can he do that and we can't? How is it they are searching our headquarters? Who does this to me? We think we will take out the old man who built the casino and all of sudden he goes home to America and gives the hotel away. To who? To Greshenko. What is this? So then what? The army comes and goes. They own the army? Our people disappear."

"They don't own the army or police. I keep telling you, it is police who are doing this, not Greshenko. He is a pawn, not a king."

"You say so, but I don't know. It doesn't sound right. These are African police. How is that possible? So, Cszepanski, do they find anything in our building? No? You are lucky they find nothing. How is that possible?"

Cszepanski shrugged. "We had a boy on the inside who is worried about his mother's health. He told us the police were coming to raid so we hid the stuff someplace else. They will be coming back, they said. One of those guys we thought were Ukrainians tells them he smelled gun oil. They will come back and tear the place apart looking for guns."

"They will not come back," Irena said as she lit a new cigarette from the stub of one she'd just smoked.

"No? Who says so? You, Irena? You have a boy on the inside, too?" Lenka waved a dismissive hand at her.

"They will not come back because they are not dense. You keep thinking they are, but you are wrong. They know there will be no guns. They are playing with us, don't you see? They are ahead of us every step of the way. Once that policeman was killed last month, they have been stalking us. They come from a long line of hunters. They will stalk their prey for days, weeks, if they have to. Before roads and buildings and civilization, they lived here and survived with wild animals in their backyards. Do you think you could step out of this hotel and live with the lions and hyenas and crocodiles? How long will you last out there, hey? You dismiss these people too quickly, Oleg. You make the mistake…okay, we make the mistake, we are thinking they would be easy marks for big tough Russian Bratva. Oleg, they are not afraid of us. Now, they are waiting for us."

"Waiting for us how?"

"Waiting for us to make the big mistake, to do another stupid thing. They are better chess players than we have been so far. Always one jump ahead of us, see? They are calling the moves. Each time we think we are going to be in charge, they do another thing, they move their bishop or maybe a pawn to a place we don't expect."

"I don't believe that. Yesterday I decided to go to the casino on the spur of the moment. I tell no one except us. We arrive and in a minute, army truck arrives. How is that done if they are calling all the moves? You are mistaken. Come on, think a minute. They are what, one, two generations from savages creeping about in nothing but a loin cloth and killing their animals with a spear? They can't know. Okay, let's say you are even halfway right, then we must do the same thing."

"Which same thing? Creep about with a spear or take over the game?"

"We will do something they don't expect."

"Like what?"

"Kill them all, the police, those men, Greshenko, the army, the whole town if we have to. We are Bratva and *We Yield to No Man!* Is that not right? It's what we say. So, we make it true. When the smoke clears, they will know what they are up against and they will fall in line, you will see."

"With respect, Chief," Cszepanski said, "that is crazy. It can't be done, and if we try, we will all find ourselves in graves in this godforsaken country. You know that. They are waiting for us to do something just like that so they can round us up, that is the ones who will have survived and are not taking a dirt nap. They slap felony arrests on us and put us in jail forever. Even if we manage to hop the border, every police agency in Africa and the world will be after us."

"So, you say quit?"

"I say, wait."

"Maybe for you. Not for Lenka. Who has an idea? Irena, dig into that brain of yours and tell us. Cszepanski, search your memory for a plan that can work here. If I don't have one soon, I swear, I will just march over to that police post with automatic pistol and just start shooting. I will keep shooting until they are all dead or I am. I will find out if I am right or I am dead. So, talk to me."

Irena and Cszepanski looked at one another. Decision time, stay or go, before Lenka kicked over the tent pole and everything collapsed and it was too late. Buy some time. That is what they understood they needed to do.

"We go after the woman," Irena said.

"What woman? There are woman police?"

"Not a woman police. We talked of this before. We put that game ranger who is policeman's woman in a bad spot and they do one of two things, okay? Either they cave in and we work out an arrangement where they leave us alone to run hotels and businesses and in return, we secure the area for them from any other problems like always. Or, this is worst case, we don't get that, but they give us a pass to leave the country clean. It is best plan."

"We tried a snatch and what happens? Our man is dead. So how do we get this woman when we missed on the daughter?"

"This time, I go get the woman. I don't fail. It is a woman thing."

"And you think this will work?"

"Look at where we are. We came to do a simple thing. Instead we are chasing our tails because these people have been able to confuse us. We go back to original plan. It works or it doesn't. That is what we came to see. So, let's see. Having a hostage will help one way and if plan fails, it buys us a safe passage out."

"Cszepanski, what do you think?"

"I think this makes sense. To do what the Davidova says is within our power. It does not require many men. We grab the right people and, like she says, it works one way or the other. Even if we have to leave, we know the ground and can come back later with better idea how to succeed. So, I say we try that."

Lenka scowled as he turned the idea over in his mind. "Okay, we go tonight. Now, Cszepanski, round up whoever we have left and get ready. Irena and me have to plan and get ready, too."

Irena knew what "getting ready" meant. She sighed and tried to conjure up an afternoon that didn't require her acquiring more bruises in uncomfortable places. She remembered the French diplomat who'd taught her a few tricks. Perhaps a little help from some vodka and those tricks will keep Oleg happy. She hoped it would. She wasn't sure she could take another round of the "usual" with Lenka.

Cszepanski had made it halfway out the door when his phone vibrated. He paused and took the call. Anyone listening would have heard was, "No? Okay, keep me in touch and call me when you're sure." Nothing more.

"Something?" Lenka asked.

"Not sure. Probably just a big mistake. I will call you if anything turns up you need to worry about."

"I am never worrying, Cszepanski. Remember that."

Chapter Forty-one

It had been a busy night. A successful one at that. Most importantly, no one had died. No one fired a shot. Only Mwambe had to exercise a modicum of force. The alert and the night had done what he could not do alone. Yet, Kgabo Modise worried. He turned to Sanderson and said, "The fat lady hasn't sung."

"What fat lady would that be? There is a large person we should be hearing? I missed something between waking up and finding you missing and lunch. What are you saying?"

"It is an expression. It means we are not done with this Lenka, that there is more to come. It is an expression from those operas written by Rra Wagner where the person singing the part of the heroine often reported for work much overweight and people who were not particularly liking operas would ask, 'When is this business over?' and their acquaintance would say, 'It's not over until—'"

"—the fat lady sings. Okay, I get it. It is not nice to dismiss women who are fighting the pounds as 'fat ladies.' Superintendent Mwambe is a fat man. If I were to say, 'It is not over until the fat man dances' what would you think?"

"I would think you were improving your sense of humor."

"Men. Always the double standard. So, Kgabo Modise, the thin policeman, who or what is your 'fat lady' today? What will constitute the singing? Lenka? That woman? She is not fat, by the way. She is very slim, like one of those snakes in Kazangula."

"It is an expression and my 'fat lady' only means I don't think we are done with these people yet. They have been badly beaten. Some of them, the police in Gaborone tell me, have been trying to leave the country. I do not think they will take this beating they are experiencing lying down."

"These men who are trying to leave the country, they think the 'fat lady' has sung?"

"Probably. So, now forget fat ladies. I am worried about what the ones who are still here will try next. I do not think they are finished with us. That Lenka, he is like an animal. If he thinks he is forced into a corner, he could be very dangerous, you see? He could go crazy mad and start shooting. There is no defense against a crazy man with a gun and lots of ammunition. By the time we would get to him, many would be dead or dying."

"And you think he would do such a crazy thing?"

"I think he could."

"What will you do?"

"Go back to work. I have people in the Mowana Lodge. I will call them in and ask if they have any ideas, if they heard anything, if they can guess."

>>>

Patience Botshabelo, her brother Andrew, Lois Moeti, and Tiki Nguyn sat in a semicircle, their notebooks open and ready. Modise had placed them in service at the lodge as soon as he'd heard that Lenka had reserved a suite. Besides Patience, who worked the bar, Andrew had been assigned to food service and in that capacity brought the endless bottles of vodka and snacks to Lenka's room. Lois did maid service. She had a great deal to report, if asked. She hoped she would not be. What she knew of this Lenka and his *nyatse* would make her stammer and blush. Tiki worked the motor pool and kept track of the comings and goings of Lenka, his woman, and others who dropped in.

None of them would admit it to the others, but they were relieved that Inspector Modise had pulled them off their duty at the lodge. Every day they feared could be their last. The Russians had seemed increasingly angry and desperate and looked at everyone with suspicion. Rumors of the Russian gangs' brutality and violence had been a daily part of their training.

"What can you tell me?" Modise asked. "Any hints as to what this man and the woman will do next?"

Patience started. "Nothing new since my last report, Inspector. In the last few days, they have avoided the bar. I think they do their drinking somewhere else now."

"In their rooms," Andrew said. "They have gone through nearly a case of expensive vodka and liters of mixes. I can only tell you, from the peek I get into the room when I take up the tray, that something is going on now. They are planning something."

"Any ideas?"

"It is risky standing outside their door. They are paranoid and will frequently jerk it open to see if anyone is listening outside."

"You did that?"

"Oh, yes. I nearly got caught, but I heard the footsteps and managed to duck into a room the cleaner, that's Lois, was working in. Most of their conversation is in Russian, of course, and mine is not so good. Anyway this last time, all I could hear was the Russian saying something about if he didn't get something—I don't know what, help, maybe. Then I am hearing he planned to shoot up the police post."

"The police post. No, he wouldn't do anything that rash. That's everything?"

"Best I could do. This man Lenka, he is very hot in the head and I think he could do almost anything. After he said what he might or would do, I can't tell which, it got too quiet. I beat a path down the corridor and out of sight."

"Lois?"

"Inspector, Modise, I can tell you that the man and the woman make great messes in their bed. It is not every night. I think the messes are the biggest when something has gone wrong."

"This morning?"

"Worst ever. The sheets were...well, there was some blood where I suppose she had...you know."

"I don't know and don't want to know. Tiki, anything?"

"Only that the SUVs is always gassed and ready. They could go at any moment. Where? Who knows? Gaborone, Harare, the airport? You can never tell with this lot."

"Okay, you four. You are not to go back to those jobs anymore. As you are describing him, Lenka seems ready to explode. The woman and the others, who knows? I don't want you there if, or when, their heads crack open. Good work."

⟩⟩⟩

"That you, Yuri?"

"Sorry, Leo, I forgot the time difference between here and Chicago. Did I get you up?"

"No problem. I don't sleep much anymore."

"How is Mrs. Painter?

"Getting better. She'll live. How about you? Things going along okay? What's Modise up to?"

"It's like a Hollywood western here, Leo. *Святейший Престол в прошлом месяце*, these cops are unreal."

"Did you just say, 'holy crap,' Yuri?"

"Something close to it. You've been studying Russian?"

"Just the cussing. I've found you can get along fine in most countries if you can cuss in their language. So, what are you saying, blasphemy aside?"

"Funny business here, Leo, that's all. Just when you think they are about to blow the whole operation, they manage to do something completely unexpected. Hell, it wouldn't surprise me if they march on Lenka with armor-plated elephants with machine guns mounted on their backs. Lenka is down to about three or four guys. The amazing thing is only one person is dead. One of their guys tried to snatch a daughter of a local woman. You remember the game ranger, Sanderson? Anyway, all that happened in Gaborone, not here. Somehow these guys are getting it done. I just hope they can last long enough to put Lenka away forever."

"I told you. Stick with the little cop. He's good. So how are you doing?"

"Good, I guess. I wonder, when all this ends, what happens to me."

"The government cut you a deal. They will keep their end of it. I suggested to Modise's boss that he ought to give you a new identity. I thought with the moniker you now have, there'd be no end to people looking for you for one reason or another, mostly bad. How does the name, Adam Neve strike you? It ought to do the trick."

"Adam Neve? You are joking with me, right?"

"Nope. New beginnings for you, Genesis and all that. So, settle in and run your hotel and casino."

"Not mine, yours."

"Nope. I won't be coming back to Botswana anymore, Yuri. I'm on a short string, they say."

"They say? Who is they and what string?"

"Doctors. Listen, I changed my will and all my interests in the casino go to you. Finish the Lenka thing and settle down. Hell, get married and have a family. Live long and prosper. Isn't that what the guy on *Star Trek* says? I can't remember who, though. Maybe the one with the pointy ears"

"Leo?"

"Cancer, Yuri. If you live long enough, it will find you. Good luck."

The line went dead. Yuri stared at the phone in his hand. Leo Painter would forever be a mystery to him. If Yuri were the crying kind, he would have shed a tear. He wasn't and so he didn't, but had he been, he would have.

It would be dark soon. He called the Americans and told them to be on the alert. Lenka might be wounded, but he still had some men. Until the cops had him in custody, no one would be safe. And everyone knew how dangerous a wounded animal could be. Yuri had lived in the dark most of his adult life, but real darkness worried him. He had not yet come to appreciate Botswana nights. In this strange land where wild animals shared your space, darkness for him was not a welcome thing. Because he worried, he stayed alert. Because he stayed alert, he survived.

Chapter Forty-two

Later, when Modise had time to work his way through the events of that night, he would wonder at how such a violent ending had evolved from his original and simple plan to spy on and then deport Lenka and his people. Perhaps it would have been clearer if he had been raised in the plains of the United States where thunderstorms can, if the conditions are right, turn into deadly tornados which will tear a path of destruction and devastation over miles of land and threaten every living thing in their way. Or, if he had lived close to the sea where the convergence of certain otherwise benign barometrics can produce the "perfect storm" that will race across miles of sea, sinking ships and even reordering the very nature of the ocean ecosystem. How was he to know that the presence of a dangerous woman in the person of Irena Davidova, the stubbornness of an American entrepreneur, the unpredictability of a wounded and betrayed hired killer, the fearlessness of an otherwise ordinary game ranger, and the heartlessness of the Bratva culture would all collide and create so much havoc in a few hectic hours on an otherwise ordinary night on the Chobe River?

It should be noted that neither he nor any of the players in the drama had any idea any of this would happen. Each, in his own orbit, moved into the arena wholly ignorant of the presence of the others. None had even an inkling of what happened elsewhere and only in the humid half light of dawn did any of them realize what had or had not occurred and their respective roles in it. Modise could only thank God that the forces of evil had been turned on themselves and the people he admired, indeed one that he loved, had survived and his precious Chobe had been cleansed. How his boss would see it was anyone's guess.

Cszepanski would be the only one who might have predicted the chaos and, when it was confirmed that someone answering to the description of Alexei Grelnikov had crossed the border from Zambia into Botswana, he knew that trouble, serious trouble, headed his way. He called Lenka to warn him. The warning ended in Lenka's voice mail. He could guess why—Irena was ministering to her baby. He left a message—and jumped into the truck which he'd kept parked outside the warehouse for just this moment. He drove as fast as he dared south to Francistown where he left the truck in the airport parking lot. Later, he would book a series of flights northward, hopping from one out-of-the-way regional airport to another and finally all the way back to Zagreb where he would disappear into the shadows of the Balkan underworld from whence he'd come.

A Lenka warned was not a Lenka prepared. Relatively refreshed and newly showered he retrieved Cszepaski's message. Irena had already left to reconnoiter the casino. Her plan, she'd said when she left, would be to snatch Modise's woman and use her to force the policeman to come to terms. The time had come to reply to them, she'd said. How much her absence played a role in what happened next cannot be determined. At any rate, without Irena's presence to moderate his subsequent actions, Lenka slipped off the rails. He grabbed two large automatics, charged out of the lodge, and headed for the warehouse. He would show them how it was done in St. Petersburg. He would take on Gur himself if it turned out that it was he who'd crossed the border. He would also have something to settle with Cszepanski who must have betrayed him in the first place when he failed to follow orders and kill Grelnikov. The Boers would watch and learn an important lesson.

He braked in front of the warehouse in a shower of flying gravel. He cocked both pistols and headed toward the door. He kicked it open, gun raised, and stepped in. One of the Boers lay dead in a pool of his own blood. The second one cowered in a corner. Gur stood over him with a length of rusty and bloody rebar. He would have beaten the brains out of this Boer as well except he was interrupted when Lenka raised one of his pistols and fired at him.

The problem with high titers of adrenaline in one's blood stream is that it tends to make your hand less steady and your actions more impetuous. If he wished to kill a man with the reputation and the size of Gur, Lenka should have known that he would have to aim very carefully and at a vital spot—someplace that would cause him to drop in his tracks. A bullet to the brain, for example, would do the trick or a well placed shot to the pubic bone which would shatter his pelvis and cause him to collapse like faulty scaffolding. A miss would be bad. But the absolute last thing he wanted to do was wound his target. That is what he did. The grazing flesh wound only stoked Gur's rage. He charged Lenka like a maddened water buffalo. Lenka never got off a second shot.

Gur had him by the throat and within a half second was shaking the life out of him. Pistols clattered across the room. Lenka clawed at Gur's face and gasped for air. With one final wrench, Gur broke his neck and flung him across the room where he landed in a crumpled heap more nearly resembling a pile of dirty laundry than the leader of a fearful Bratva organization. Gur stood, hands on hips, his breathing ragged, and watched the life wink out in Lenka's eyes. Then, he picked up one of the discarded pistols, spun, and shot the second Boer in the back of his head as he attempted to crawl out the door.

〉〉〉

Irena had managed to corral Sanderson as she left her office at the Game Park. Sanderson was about to say something until she saw the shiny automatic in the Russian's hand accompanied by a flinty look in her eyes. Instead, she did as the woman demanded while wondering at her own apparent lack of fear. Perhaps it was the result of facing down truly fierce predators as part of her almost daily routine. Against a hungry circling lion or a pack of hyenas, this woman was pretty small potatoes. That was when she remembered what, or more accurately, who, this woman reminded her of: Kotsi Mosadi! This Russian woman was a hyena. But where Kotsi Mosadi's viciousness was innate and expected, this bad woman had acquired it as an alternative to a life lived in the light. Sanderson would mourn the death of Kotsi Mosadi. She would not shed any tears for this one. So, she thought, if the lioness could take down Danger Woman, she could take down this evil person. Modise had said she was a *tau*, didn't he? But how?

Irena forced Sanderson to drive her to the warehouse.

"We use your truck. No one will question you driving in a game ranger truck."

Sanderson led her to the Land Rover which had still not had its doors replaced. She gritted her teeth remembering that she'd sent several reminders to the maintenance people to have them replaced on the machine and Michael said he would do it. She thought of her son and of his friend, Sekgele. Not friend, intended. She might never see either of them again. The thought made her sad and then angry. She would not let this evil woman win. She would survive this night. She smiled.

"Something is funny with you?"

"No, not funny. I'm sorry, Missus, but this is the only vehicle available. Be sure to buckle the seat belt."

"You think I am stupid? Of course I buckle."

They drove to the warehouse. As they approached it, they saw Gur lurch away into the night holding his side. Irena muttered something in Russian which Sanderson assumed was a curse. Several curses, in fact. Apparently the large man was not a welcome sight. She was made to drive right up to the door. Irena had her dismount and precede her into the front office. They took in the carnage, the two dead Boers and the grotesque shape that used to be Oleg Lenka in the corner. Irena gasped and then headed for the phone and banged in a number.

"Bart," she shouted, "Do you know who is talking to you? Yes? Good. You have a pickup over here. When? Now, is when. You go to the river and do it now. Look for the signal in the usual place."

Sanderson realized at that moment that all of the things Modise had told her about these gangsters were as bad as he'd said. These were very evil people. Irena, motioned for Sanderson to stand in a corner while she spun the dial and opened the safe. She grabbed everything in it, dollars, pula, rubles, papers, passports, and stuffed them all into a small duffel.

"Okay, game ranger woman, you are now driving me to the river. Through the park, to the river. Quick, you hear? Now move."

Sanderson did as she was told. They entered the park and she started down the river road. After a minute or so, she began to accelerate. A little at first, then more so.

"Not so fast, you. Slow down."

"It is best if we go fast, Missus. If we drive too slowly, the animals can run and catch us and you don't want that. See, we have no doors. A lion could drag you out. You know about that woman in South Africa." Sanderson had the truck moving as fast as she dared. "Is your seat belt latched?"

"I say to slow down. Of course belt is latched. Slow down or I shoot."

"No, I don't think you should do that. If you do that, we wreck. Then what?"

"Not shoot? We'll see." Irena pulled the trigger and shot Sanderson in her left leg.

The truck swerved, skidded, and nearly tipped over. The pain was not as bad as she imagined it might be. Endorphins, she'd heard, would do that. Anyway, the pain would come later, she guessed. Right now, she was pumping epinephrine into her system at an alarming rate. She got the truck righted and back on the track. Once again she stamped on the accelerator. She knew Irena would not dare shoot her again. She'd nearly killed them both the first time. She hoped the bullet had not nicked an artery. If so, neither of them were going to see the river. As she approached the ridge, she braced herself against the seat back, gripped the steering wheel with both hands, arms locked. The next second, the truck lurched violently to the right. Irena was thrown against Sanderson and before she could grab anything, the truck lurched back to the left. Irena sailed out into the night. Her gun flew out of her hand and clattered to the truck's floor. The Land Rover bounced once, twice, slid sideways and continued down the track, but more slowly as its motor stalled.

Back up the track, Sanderson could hear Irena cursing at her. The darkness closed in and then she heard a scream of terror. Then silence. A second later the quiet was shattered by the angry roaring of lions fighting over a new kill. She held her breath. She knew a new lion kill might attract other predators. She heard nothing stirring in her immediate area. She retrieved the pistol from under the seat and placed it on the bench beside her. She attempted to restart the SUV's engine. She gritted her teeth and after the third try, she managed to get the motor running, the SUV in gear, and moving. Something had come detached from the underside of the truck. She followed a circuitous path away from the lions and back toward the park gate. Because her left leg had stopped responding to orders from her brain, she made the trip in low gear dragging whatever it was that had come undone from the chassis, and with Irena's pistol at the ready.

Chapter Forty-three

Gur was only vaguely aware of the car that drove up as he left the warehouse. His mind and footsteps were set on a course to find Greshenko, the second party to his earlier humiliation and betrayal. When he finished with him, he'd find that Harry person, the Davidova, and then he'd be done. He gasped for air. The exertion of manhandling Lenka had aggravated his wounds. The doctors had been right. His broken ribs had not knit sufficiently and tore at his lungs again. They, in turn, were filling with his blood. Not fast, but inexorably. He staggered down the road toward the casino. Greshenko would be there, he was sure of that. He would be there and he, Gur, would tear him apart. It was the promise he'd made to himself a week ago and one he fully intended to keep. Ten paces from the casino office door he bellowed Greshenko's name and followed it with a string of obscenities in Russian guaranteed to bring his enemy outdoors.

Greshenko did hear him and glanced out the window to see if he had heard correctly. He had. No one would ever call Greshenko a coward, not and live. Neither would they call him a fool and no one but a fool would face off with a maddened, and armed Grelnikov. Yuri slipped out a side door and headed toward the river. Someone…Lenka's stooge? Who knew? Someone called out that Greshenko was headed away. Gur broke into a staggering jog toward the voice.

"He is going to the river," the voice said.

Gur saw the man pointing at the retreating figure of Greshenko. He paused and shot the man on the spot and then careened on his way.

Yuri made sure he stayed out of range of the man on his heels. He knew Gur did not want to shoot him. Not right away. He wanted to punish him first. Greshenko understood this. It was the Bratva way. He could also hear the labored breathing behind him and reckoned that if he could outlast his pursuer, Gur would soon drop. When that happened, he'd be able to incapacitate Gur once and for all. He drifted through the shadows and down to the riverbank. He could hear snorting off shore. A pod of hippos must be nearby. Greshenko paused. A bulky form heaved itself from the river and waddled inland as Gur crashed through the brush and down onto the riverbank. There he stopped to get his bearings. He had wandered too far to the edge and now stood between the hippo and the water. The hippo wheeled, lowered its head, and stared red eyed at the man blocking the way back to his pod. Gur fired a shot at the animal. In less time than Greshenko had to voice a warning, the hippo was on the big Russian. He disappeared under the animal's bulk.

While it is generally acknowledged that hippopotami are vegetarians, it is also known that on occasion, they will eat flesh. At the same time it is also possible that Gur's body was simply dragged into the river and left to the tiger fish. In any event, except for a nine millimeter automatic with his fingerprints on it and a shoe, no trace of Gur was found the following day. Or ever.

The remains of Irena Davidova were identified with greater certainty. They consisted of a fresh female skeleton with its skull pretty much intact, some odd bits of torn and bloody clothing, and pieces of jewelry, all scattered over a few square meters. DNA testing eventually confirmed the identification. Also, an intact duffle bag filled with money and passports turned up five meters further down the road.

The lions had moved on to a different area in the park.

◇◇◇

The director of the DIS called Modise on the carpet. He had a problem to solve. On the one hand, the success of the operation in the Chobe could not be denied. Not only had they ridded the country of a nascent threat from one gang of criminals, but the way in which it had been accomplished sent a clear and unequivocal message that any new threat from persons with similar ideas would not work. The word in the dark reaches of the underworld from St. Petersburg to Tokyo to Cali was clear. In Botswana they do not shoot poachers on sight but they do not treat them kindly either. Mobsters, gangs, and organized crime were considered poachers.

On the other hand, Modise had broken nearly every rule in the book. He had committed resources without proper authorization. He had misrepresented the situation in Kasane and had acted in a manner not in accordance with proper police protocol. There was no room in the Botswana Police force for a cowboy. As much as the world seemed to admire this peculiarly American phenomenon, police work in the country would follow correct procedure and practice.

The director had Kgabo stand in front of his desk for what must have seemed an hour but could have been no more than a few minutes. Finally he looked up and stared at him. He lit a cigarette. Modise felt a trickle of sweat run down his back.

"Terrible habit, Modise. I hope you do not smoke."

"No, sir."

"Good. You know how I feel about the image this unit has?"

"Yes, sir, I believe I do. No smoking."

"No, yes, no. I am not speaking of smoking, Inspector."

"No, sir. You are speaking of the operation."

"Exactly. Very well. Then, you know that there is no room in it for men and women working alone. You are familiar with the American story of the Lone Ranger?"

"Ah, no, sir. Did he work in a game preserve?"

"Come, come, Modise. It says in you dossier that you spent time with the American FBI. That is correct, yes?"

"Yes, sir."

"And in all that time you never ran across the Lone Ranger?"

"No, sir. Sorry."

"Hmmm…John Wayne?"

"Yes, sir. The Duke."

"Good. Then we understand each other."

"Sir?"

"Modise, I do not want any Wild West, shoot-'em-up cowboys in this unit. Is that clear?"

"Ah. Yes, sir. Crystal clear, no cowboys."

"Very well. Now, let me be absolutely clear, what you accomplished up there on the river was extraordinary. It was not to form, it was…Modise, it was insane. You realize that if it had failed, if there had been any unnecessary bloodshed, you would be walking a beat out in Salt Pans for the rest of your life. And no Superstar Taylor Swift and her *Wildest Dreams* to keep you company out there, you understand. Or any of your wildest dreams either. Modise, I cannot let these breaches of protocol pass without doing something about it, you see?"

"No, sir…umm…Yes, sir. I am sorry, but—" Modise saw his career sliding away. His heart sank.

The director spun a quarter turn in his swivel chair and stared at the wall for a moment. Modise glanced in the same direction. The wall was blank. He swiveled back. "On the other hand, you damned well did it, didn't you?"

"Sir?"

The director shuffled papers on his desk and cleared his throat again. Modise swallowed. His career teetered on a precipice.

"Very well. Inspector Modise, for your success I am promoting you to a superintendent's position. At the same time, you do understand, I cannot let the unauthorized use of equipment and men go unnoticed or accounted for."

Promoted to superintendent? "No sir, I suppose not."

"You suppose…Yes, well." The director frowned and tapped a sheet of paper with a forefinger. "Thanks to the good offices of Joseph Ikanya and, I gather, some other things that happened up there, Superintendent Motsu Mwambe has put in his retirement papers which, it turns out, is a fortuitous happenstance, as you will soon realize." The director cleared his throat again, reshuffled the papers on the desk, and looked up, his expression stern. "Therefore, Modise, for your failure to follow orders and for the blatant misuse of the abovementioned resources, I am assigning you to Kasane as its new superintendent. I hope this will be an object lesson to you and for the remainder of the force as well, to witness and learn from. Dismissed."

Modise couldn't be sure, but he would later report to Sanderson when he visited her in the hospital, that he was pretty sure he saw a twinkle in the director's eye when he'd exiled him to the Chobe.

Author's Notes

First, three comments:

1) Despite what you might have heard to the contrary, there is no standing order, policy, mandate, or understanding in Botswana that poachers are to be shot on sight, either when caught in the act, while trying to flee, or any other circumstances except should they shoot first. The notion that the Botswana Defense Force would shoot at poachers is a rumor. Some might say a convenient one, but a rumor, nonetheless.

2) That said, it should be emphasized that poaching in Botswana is a serious crime and those who engage in it will be and are prosecuted to the fullest extent of the law. The President of Botswana at the time of this writing, His Excellency Ian Khama Seretse Khama, is a serious conservationist. He is the driving force behind the program to reestablish rhinos in the country. Protection of the animals in the various game parks is a high priority of his and the government.

3) There are no Russian mobsters lurking about the country or organized crime, generally. Botswana is one of the least corrupt countries in the world. It is a modern democracy with serious politicians dedicated to the advancement of its people and progress with restraint.

Also, Botswana has the largest population of elephants of any country. I guess that makes four comments.

Glossary

Setswana is a dialect of Bantu, as is Zulu, and many other languages spoken in sub-Saharan Africa. The stem is, Tswana
+ Ba…people of the…*Ba*tswana
+ Bo…the country of the…*Bo*tswana
+ Mo…a person of…*Mo*tswana
+ Se…language of…*Se*tswana

Some Phrases and Words that Appear in the Text

A re tsamaye! = Let's go!

Bakkie = Africaans' word for pickup truck

Boikobo =obedient

Botsolano = friendship

Botshabelo = refuge, sanctuary

*Combi*e = small bus or van

Dumela…hello + *Mma, Rra* = ma'am, sir

Gabz = a contraction for Gaborone

Kgopa = snail

Kgosi = chief

Kgosi Mosadi = woman chief

Kgotla = courtyard, meeting place

Kotsi = danger

Lekgwamolelo = volcano

Manong = vultures

Mmegi = Local newspaper which has an online edition, if you happen to be interested in the affairs of Botswana

Mma (pronounced mah) = Mrs., as a title of respect

Modimo = God

Moeti = visitor

Moloi = witch, deviner

Monontsha = fertilizer

Moshutele = manure

Mosekisi = prosecutor, judge

Mosadi = woman

Motsu = sharp point, arrow

Mowa = soul, breath (of life)

Nkuku = grandmother

No mathata = no problem, no worries

Ntate = father

Nyatse = paramour, mistress

O tsogile jang = How are you?

Panel beaters = auto body shop

Phane = fried or cooked caterpillars, considered a delicacy

Pula (literally rain) = the currency of Botswana and *Thebe* (shield) = coinage

Pheri = hyena + di/du, *dupheri* = hyenas

Rra (pronounced rah) = Mr. or sir (with respect)

Rre (pronounced ray) = Father, and designates a superior type of Mr., usually a clergyman

Rremogolo = grandfather

Rondeval = a circular hut fashioned from mud and woven branches, with a thatch roof

Sala sentle = Stay well...goodbye

Sekgele = prize

Tau = lion, + *di* = lions

Tshedisa molewane = banished

Tumelo = faith

See also: http://en.wickipedia.org/wiki/Tswana_language.

HAART = Highly Active Antiretroviral Therapy

Kazangula is a village in Botswana on the Chobe River which boasts, among other things, a snake sanctuary or exhibit.

Setswana is the traditional language of Botswana. The official language is English.

Having alternative languages for specific purposes is a practice not limited to Botswana. We in the United States would do well to consider it as well, at least conceptually. Think of how much anger goes out of the system when we allow that, for example, the southwest has a "traditional language"—Spanish, and an official language—English.

Whereas Gaborone is pronounced with the G as a guttural ch (as in *loch)*, the contraction, Gabz, has a hard G. People from South Africa pronounce Gaborone with a hard G, however.

People are often greeted attaching the names of their firstborn with the appropriate title, i.e. my wife would be Mma Julie and I might be Rra Jeff.

The religious configuration is predominantly Christian (62 percent Protestant, 5.0 percent Roman Catholic). Indigenous religions constitute 23 percent; Islam, 0.3 percent; and Hindu, 0.15 percent.

The following has been lifted from Botswana's official website:

> *The Republic of Botswana is situated in Southern Africa, nestled between South Africa, Namibia, Zimbabwe, and Zambia. The country is democratically ruled, boasts a growing economy and a stable political environment. Botswana has some of Africa's last great wildernesses including the famous Okavango Swamps and the Kalahari Desert.*

Botswana is the largest exporter of gemstone diamonds in the world as well as a large beef exporter to the European Union.

For more information about this fascinating country go to www. gov.bw.

NB: In some Slavic language groups, the combination Cs is pronounced as Sh. It is often written in reverse: Sc. What you do with a z juxtaposed next to that is up to you. I once had a man working for me whose surname had that combination and when I asked how to pronounce his name, he said, "Just call me Phil."

To receive a free catalog of Poisoned Pen Press titles, please provide your name, address, and email address in one of the following ways:

Phone: 1-800-421-3976
Facsimile: 1-480-949-1707
Email: info@poisonedpenpress.com
Website: www.poisonedpenpress.com

Poisoned Pen Press
6962 E. First Ave. Ste 103
Scottsdale, AZ 85251

CPSIA information can be obtained at www.ICGtesting.com
Printed in the USA
LVOW08s2056090616

491951LV00004BA/202/P